To Tom Berry
Wang Ling

The Little Phoenix

Wang Ling

VANTAGE PRESS
New York

FIRST EDITION

All rights reserved, including the right of
reproduction in whole or in part in any form.

Copyright © 2000 by Wang Ling

Published by Vantage Press, Inc.
516 West 34th Street, New York, New York 10001

Manufactured in the United States of America
ISBN: 0-533-13296-7

Library of Congress Catalog Card No.: 99-96650

0 9 8 7 6 5 4 3 2 1

To Dr. Muriel Fleit
and
Ling Ling

Contents

Prologue	1
1. Chen Shau Feng Arrives	15
2. Fong Syang Hwa's Birthday Party	25
3. Graduation	38
4. America and Ohio	43
5. In Ohio	48
6. Plainfield College and the China House	56
7. The Plainfield Lions	73
8. Football Season	93
9. Champs	120
10. The Finale	143

The Little Phoenix

Prologue

For Lee Chen, the third day of August, 1974, was not just another day, as it was for most people, it was his seventieth birthday. After rising early as was his custom, the retired actor began his daily exercise routine. Since his housekeeper had not yet arrived, he returned to the back yard to perform sword-and-cudgel exercises before attending to his daily ablutions. He was shaving, just as he did every day, when he heard the front door slam shut, signaling the arrival of Mrs. Kang. He knew she'd be busy for a while in the kitchen, and so he finished his toilet at a leisurely pace, dressed and readied himself, and went into the dining room to read the newspaper Mrs. Kang had left for him. A few minutes later, she entered, carrying Lee's breakfast and a birthday cake. A broad smile appeared on her face as she handed Lee a telegram:
"Good morning, sir....Happy birthday."
"Thank you, Mrs. Kang," Lee responded, putting down the paper and reading the telegram:
"Happy birthday, Father. Long life—Live to a hundred years! From Sher-sher and Charles."
It was pleasing to Lee that his daughter always remembered his birthday. After his breakfast, to which a slice of birthday cake had been added, he asked Mrs. Kang to take the rest of the cake home to her grandchildren. Later, Lee phoned for a cab to drive him to the cemetery. Visiting the grave of his second wife, Lavender, was a ritual the actor always performed on his birthday.

After lunch, carrying a carton of wine, Lee left his house for the Shan Tung Country Men's Association in order to invite his friends and countrymen to have a celebratory drink with him. This gathering place had been established by Chinese who came from the province of Shan Tung, China, in 1949. In the association, the countrymen could speak their own dialect and observe their own culture in Hong Kong. What was most important to some people who came to this place was hearing news of their loved ones from behind the Bamboo Curtain and overseas. At Lee's entrance, everyone in the hall gave the popular retired actor a standing ovation. Lee removed the wine bottles from the carton and asked everyone to join him. They toasted his health and wished him a long life. He was well respected among the employees and patrons of the association, who were familiar with Lee's background. Members of Lee's family had fought against the Japanese and the Communists. During his active days, Lee had had a strong, loyal following. He had been the most popular opera star in China before his escape in 1949. In Hong Kong, he was not only a renowned Chinese opera star, but starred prominently in movies and television. Since his retirement, it was Lee's habit to go to the association three times a week to socialize with his countrymen.

The toasting completed, Lee spotted his old friend Lao Tsao, sitting alone in the back of the hall eating peanuts and drinking tea.

While a prisoner of the Communists, Lao Tsao had been brutally tortured and, as a result, had lost his sight. Lao Tsao, who had been strong and sharp in his youth, was now bent from age and a life of hardship. His hands and face were covered with scars as a reminder of his capture. Lee and Lao Tsao had come from the same village in Shan Tung and together had fought the Japanese during World War II. Lee had not been a partisan, but Lao Tsao had been active as an intelligence officer in the Koumingtang regime and been arrested by the Communists in 1949. The following year, with the help of Koumingtang undercover agents, Lao Tsao had escaped from mainland China and found a home in Hong Kong.

Lao Tsao could be found at the association hall any time of day, seated at the same corner table. He lived in a room upstairs and acted as a token watchman for the association. The blind man was a focal point for people to come to, to learn about what had happened to their relatives or friends. A great portion of Lao Tsao's work was giving and receiving information, and on one wall of the association hall was a large bulletin board, where people could leave messages or notes.

Carrying a bottle of wine, Lee crossed the room to Lao Tsao's table, gently putting a hand on the old man's arm. In a cheerful voice, Lao Tsao greeted his old friend.

"Happy birthday, Lee. Do you feel any older?"

"Yes, I feel a thousand years old."

"What, no change?" As they sipped their wine, both men had a laugh at the joke they had shared for years. They swapped a few stories about the "good old" military days. The wine made Lee a little giddy, and he rose to entertain the assemblage with some old favorite songs and scenes from the Chinese opera. This was his way of repaying his friends and fans for having been so loyal to him all these years. It was also an opportunity for him to use his talents as a performer, skills which had so long lain dormant. A short time later, he said good-bye to all his good friends and left for home to prepare for his seventieth birthday party, the event he had been looking forward to for many weeks.

At 7:00 P.M. sharp that evening, Mr. Fong, one of Lee's business partners, arrived at Lee's home to chauffeur him to a fashionable restaurant, where Lee's current friends and associates were giving the party.

Except for Lee's white hair, and a hint of bags under his eyes, he looked the same as the day he had touched base in Hong Kong in 1949. There were over a hundred people at the party, and it was a moving experience for him to be so honored by his associates and admirers. The celebration lasted until midnight, when a very tired but happy Lee Chen rose to say farewell. A chorus of a hundred voices chanted, "Happy birthday, long life." Fong felt a sense of satisfaction as he escorted Lee to his car. He admired Master Chen and looked up to him, because he was rich and popular, and, by being associated with Master Chen, Mr. Fong also became popular.

At home again, Lee leaned back in his favorite wicker chair on the front porch. He removed his jacket, replacing it with a thin silk one. The night was warm, without a breeze, yet Lee kept his jacket on because he never felt fully dressed without it. The old man gazed at the sky with the bright moon overhead. His eyes followed the lights of an airplane as it moved across the sky from east to west. He lit a cigar and let his thoughts drift to events of long ago. His greatest pleasure these days was ruminating about the old times.

Back then, Lee had been living in his late father's residence with his wife Grace; his mother, Yutse; his elder son, Lo; and his younger son, Agile. It was December 2, 1949, in Beijing. Lee (the star performer of the Beijing Chinese opera group) was invited to give a solo performance at a dinner for several high-ranking Communist officials. The Chen family had been Chinese Opera performers for generations. As an actor, Lee Chen needed the Communists' goodwill and support, so that he could continue to perform on the stage. He couldn't afford to snub anyone, especially those in power.

Many important people had been invited to that dinner on December 2, 1949. General Chou, a three-star general in the Red Army and a senior representative of the Communist Party, had been called away on official business at the last moment, and so his son, Ho Ho, had come on behalf of his absent father. He had come unwillingly, as he had a bitter resentment against Lee Chen.

The dinner tables were arranged in a horseshoe in front of the small stage. General Yip and his young wife sat next to Ho Ho, in front of the absent general's bodyguards. Yip had grown up in the same village and been educated at the same school as Lee Chen, in Shan Tung province. Feeling pride in his friend and countryman's achievement, General Yip talked enthusiastically of Master Chen's

Kung Fu, completely unaware of Ho Ho's seething resentment. Ho Ho mumbled to himself, "Why do people brag about Lee Chen, when everyone knows I am last year's Kung Fu champion?" Ho Ho's mother had warned him before leaving the house not to show jealousy of Master Chen and made him promise to behave himself at the party. As an extra precaution, she had sent two bodyguards with her son.

The audience warmed up to Master Chen's magnificent performance with a stamping of their feet, cries of approval, and much clapping of the hands. Sitting across from Lee and watching the audience's enthusiastic response, Ho Ho had his anger fanned to a point where he ignored his mother's admonition. He began behaving erratically, shouting at Master Chen.

"To me, you are a nothing! I can beat you with one hand tied behind my back." Lee, not wanting to engage the youth in a fight, tried to calm him with a broad smile. But Ho Ho became belligerent and stood up. Again, Lee tried to appease the young man. He told Ho Ho that he didn't want to contest him, since Ho Ho was a recognized national champion with much honor. In reality, Lee knew that, should there be a fight, he could end up shot or in prison. Should they not fight, and Ho Ho's father learn of his actions at the party, the young man would be shipped off to his grandfather in the south. Ho Ho would not be mollified. Using the back of his left hand, he swept platters of food off the table, littering the floor. Off came his Mao jacket. His father's bodyguards' attempts to restrain him proved no match for his superior skill, and they retreated. The senior party leader shouted at Ho Ho to leave, but instead Ho Ho vaulted over the table and came fast at Lee, who warded off the blows. Ho Ho struck viciously at Lee's vital points. Lee Chen, realizing he couldn't block every blow, jabbed the youth's forehead with the fingertips of his right hand. Ho Ho retreated with a visible welt on his brow. This was the first time anyone had ever struck him in a fight. He spat on the palms of his hands and doubled his efforts by switching to the tiger form to attack Lee. With fists and feet lashing out, Lee employed the gymnastic prowess of the monkey style, backflipping away from the youth. Ho Ho quickly followed the actor. Lee ceased going backwards and rolled forward, kicking the youth in the chest from the floor. The impact lifted Ho Ho into the air, and he landed flat on his back, pain showing on his face as he rubbed his chest. There was a moment of resignation, when the contestants locked eyes. Master Chen slowly shook his head to indicate to Ho Ho that the fight was over. General Chou's bodyguards came to help Ho Ho to his feet and asked Master Chen to forgive the drunken boy. Ho Ho looked around the room, saw the laughing faces, and with his eyes pleaded for help. Getting no response, he shook his fist with fury and managed to grab a pistol from one of the bodyguards. People screamed and ran for cover as Ho Ho pointed the pistol at Lee and fired. Lee leaped backwards over the table behind him, hit the floor, and rolled away from the point where he had landed. The long tablecloth hid Lee from Ho Ho's view. The young man fired in the direction where he thought Lee might be hiding. He shouted, "Bastard, I'll kill you!" Lee removed a small knife, which he carried inside his boot, and rose to his feet. Ho Ho saw him and pointed his pistol at Lee to fire again. Before squeezing the trigger, he noticed that Master Chen's left wrist was flexed.

"Damn it!" he muttered. Quickly the young combatant stepped to his right, only to lose his balance. His foot had come down on a spot where there was some food spilled on the floor, and he slipped. In an attempt to gain his balance, Ho Ho tilted his body to the left. Out came his hand to break his fall. The small knife pierced Ho Ho's throat. There was a blood-chilling scream as the bullet struck the ceiling. It was an experience any Kung Fu master wished never to face. It was Lee's intention to disarm Ho Ho, not to kill him, but, despite all efforts to revive him, he lay dead. To Lee this was a tragedy from which he would never recover.

On the night of Lee's seventieth birthday on August 3, 1974, outside the gate of Lee's property at 71 Queens Court, on Victoria

Peak, Hong Kong, a man was walking up and down the street very slowly, trying to conceal himself on this bright moonlit night. As he anticipated walking to the front gate of Lee Chen's house, he could feel fear permeating his body. Cold sweat dampened his brow, and fear dried his mouth and filled his stomach with butterflies.

His elder sister had sent him to meet Lee Chen, whom she had described in the minutest detail so there would be no mistake in recognition. It was crucial for the man to give the Chen family-recognition sign at just the right moment.

"Why," he lamented, "couldn't my elder sister have sent a more courageous person for this assignment? What if my sequence is off, or if I don't make the recognition sign fast enough? Will Master Chen kill me before I have a chance to explain?" What terrified the man was the stories he had heard at home, that Master Chen was a killer who was proficient in five fighting styles, adept at throwing small, razor-sharp knives with deadly accuracy, and capable of killing a Chinese Communist without so much as a backward glance.

The man knew he wasn't really a coward. He had come from an old, traditional Chinese heritage, which had been isolated from the modern world. He had been taught to be valiant and fearless when confronted by an aggressive enemy, preferring death to living in shame as a coward. For a moment, he considered caving in to his fear, but he knew intuitively that running away wasn't an acceptable choice. He thrust the negative thoughts from his mind and mentally rehearsed the recognition sign. By visually fantasizing a calm and peaceful meeting with no unexpected attack on his person, he was able to take back control of his body. He pushed himself away from the tree and, without pausing, walked hurriedly to the entrance. He grabbed the bars of the gate with his hands shoulder-high and chest-wide. This was the introduction sign of the Chen family. The man's name was Pa Hu, and his visit would effect a profound change on Lee's life.

Lee, who had been dozing, suddenly awoke with a start, his eyes focusing on the man passing his gate. Lee did not feel in immediate danger and continued his reflections on the past. He recalled with humor the moviemakers who had sold him on the idea of acting in fighting films. The money had been good, and it had been fun. While making these types of films, he had received much acclaim, had had many fans and admirers, and had met many people, including a strikingly beautiful young woman half his age, whom Lee had fallen in love with almost at first sight. He had wooed her ardently for several months, when what he longed for had happened: She accepted his marriage proposal.

Lavender, his second wife, had possessed an enormous business sense and an astute knowledge of the financial market. Lavender had advised her husband to produce his own films and to invest in commercial ventures. She certainly had the Midas touch, and Lee had made huge profits from taking her advice. More than that, however, she was a warm and sensitive woman, and he loved her dearly. Thinking about her brought tears to his eyes, and almost instantly a picture of his daughter, Sher Sher, came to mind.

Wasn't it five years ago that the girl had left Hong Kong for America? Sher Sher had inherited her mother's business acumen and her last wish was for her daughter to be educated in America. The girl had been eighteen at the time. Four years later, she had graduated from college with an M.B.A. and met and married an American ex–football player, Charles Lemar. Lee had never warmed up to him, partly because he wasn't Chinese and partly because he had spirited Sher Sher away from him. There were many good Chinese young men whom she could have married, either in America or in Hong Kong.

"What do I care if the big man is a retired professional football Hall-of-Famer!" thought Lee. "If the big man is so strong, why is he unable to produce an heir? Sher Sher said I was grumpy, ill tempered, and surly for no reason at all. Well, I have my reasons. Let him get to know my people, my culture and heritage. It's my daughter's smarts, not Charles's money, that has made them a financial power in Ohio." Lee slowly allowed his temper to subside.

Lee's senses tingled as the man who had passed twice before was now at the front gate. He displayed a Chen family introduction sign. Chen heard, "Sir, are you Chen Lee from Beijing?"

"Yes, I am."

Pa Hu counted slowly, one, two, three, four, five.... "I'm Pa Hu from Shan Tung." Exhausted from the effort, Pa Hu wiped his brow with the back of his left sleeve.

"Three fled, One remains, One is dead...." He released his grip on the bars and showed his open palms to Lee. Using a finger, he wrote, on his left palm, the Chen clan sign for help. Lee pushed himself to his feet, his eyes never straying from Pa Hu's face. Walking to the gate, Lee requested Pa Hu to step back. Once the man had moved backwards, he was clearly visible in the streetlight. Pa Hu was short and stout and had dark hair, an oval face, and small ears close to his head. He, in turn, stared at Lee. Everything checked, white hair, tall, muscular body, aristocratic appearance, handsome face, and fierce eyes. Lee opened the gate to let Pa Hu in. Once inside, Pa Hu followed close behind Lee. Lee went to the table and sat with his back toward the house. Nervousness shot through Pa Hu's body as he sat opposite Lee. It caused him to rehearse several Chen clan-recognition signs. Finally Pa Hu remembered to place both palms flat against the tabletop. Lee watched, with anger rising. He became impatient, and, without thinking, he reached inside his jacket pocket. That action induced immediate terror in Pa Hu, and he attempted to defend himself from the imagined attack by rising. This exertion resulted in his falling backwards, taking the chair along with him, until it hit the porch post. Up came both of his hands, waving like fans in order to forestall an attack. Pa Hu shut his eyes, preparing for the worst. After what seemed like an interminable moment, he carefully opened an eye and saw Lee wipe the perspiration from his face with a handkerchief. A shaky laugh escaped from Pa Hu's lips.

"Forgive my behavior, sir. At home, the old folks still talked about your famous flying knives, which took many Japanese lives during the war. I was expecting those flying knives to fly at me." Pa Hu rose up and carried the chair back to the table, all the while feeling Lee's eyes piercing him. Once more he sat down. This time, Pa Hu spread apart the fingers of both his hands on the tabletop. He raised his face to look at Lee, then turned over his left hand. This indicated to Lee that Pa Hu was representing Lee's son, Agile. Master Chen's face remained expressionless. As he casually reached for his glass, without putting it to his lips, he spilled some of its contents on the porch, signifying that Pa Hu was allowed to continue delivering the message. To Lee's utter amazement, Pa Hu said, "Two people have a problem. The monk who walks with his nose in a book told your son, Agile, and his wife, Butterfly, that their daughter, Shau Feng, required handling in a special way, which is beyond their means." Lee couldn't believe his ears. A clan message being delivered orally? This was unthinkable! Then he nodded his head.

"Oh, how very clever is Madam Yang. Her wisdom is profound. She selected the perfect messenger to send to me. This man's face is an open book, communicating his inner feelings. How could one distrust someone whose behavior mirrors his mind? A female child, my granddaughter, is being offered by my son, Agile, for safekeeping." Lee puffed on the cigar, pondering the information.

"That monk whom Pa Hu was referring to compiles horoscopes. He was the same monk who predicted my destiny and gave me this jade Buddha I always wear around my neck. Do I want the responsibility of rearing another girl child? On the other hand, how can I deny my son?" Pa Hu said nothing, but beads of sweat appeared on his brow. Lee removed the cigar from his mouth, placing it on the edge of the ashtray. He picked up the glass and gulped down all the liquid. The glass was set on its side on the table with the rim facing Pa Hu. A look of complete happiness exploded across Pa Hu's face as he perceived the sign. Pa Hu was on his feet. He bowed to Lee many times.

"Master Chen, I shall return in a season."

Lee replied, "Thank you, Mr. Hu. Have a safe trip home and a speedy return."

After Pa Hu's departure, Lee entered his house and headed straight for the bedroom. He felt in conflict.

"This could truly be an act of God, to have my granddaughter come to me. Still, it could be an elaborate plot hatched by General Chou's group." He lit three joss sticks, and, gesturing to the picture of his wife, Lavender, on the wall, he said, "Wife, in a few short months, this house could once again echo with a child's laughter and the sound of little steps. Agile, my youngest son, is sending me my granddaughter, Shau Feng. Remember what I used to tell you about Chen women? They are kind, intelligent, stubborn as mules, and they have strong personalities and gentle souls." Lee smiled, thinking of his own mother. Then he answered as if he heard his late wife's voice.

"Yes, I should call Sher Sher for advice." With alacrity, the old man punched a number into the phone and waited as it rang. On the other end of the line, a voice said, "Lemar Enterprises, Executive Office, Miss Koo speaking."

Lee responded in Chinese, "This is Lee Chen. I would like to speak to my daughter, Mrs. Lemar, please."

"Right away, Mr. Chen. Happy Birthday, sir."

"Thank you, Miss Koo."

There were several clicks before a voice, speaking Chinese, asked, "Father, are you all right?"

"Yes, I have something to tell you. I need your advice." Carefully Sher Sher listened to the tone of her father's voice, hoping to sense his true feeling about the little girl who was to appear from Red China to live with him. Encouraged by Lee's excitement about the prospect, Sher Sher quickly agreed that the little girl would provide new interest and delight in her father's life. Lee hung up the phone, pleased at having such an understanding and loving daughter. "Sometimes daughters bring more joy to one's old age than sons," mused Lee, as he sat back on the chair, puffing on his cigar. In the back of Lee's mind lurked the thought of a possible General Chou retaliation scheme. Lee carried his throwing knives on him to protect himself against a possible attack. The actor employed the same precautions in his house that he had always taken during his guerrilla days.

Numerous misgivings about taking his granddaughter to live with him continued to flood his mind. As a result, many midnight phone conversations occurred with Sher Sher about Shau Feng. He moaned, "At my age, I'm too old to rear a child, especially a girl, who needs female guidance. What if I should die before she reaches adulthood?" Sher Sher countered, "Nonsense, Father, you aren't senile or feeble. You reared me without a female. Father, don't worry so much. I will take over should you die. I shall do my duty even if it means I must fight with Charles over the child." Sher Sher wasn't being truthful with her father. She had told him several white lies. One was that Charles preferred male children. Another one was that they had been trying for years to have a child of their own. But the real reason that frightened Sher Sher was the early death of her own mother, Lavender. She couldn't stand the thought of dying young and leaving a young child alone on earth without a caring mother. Repeatedly Sher Sher had asked her father to have her old room repainted for Shau Feng as soon as possible. Sher Sher also asked her father to have Bright Star, her old doll, reconditioned for the little girl. Finally, she suggested having Shau Feng's horoscope compiled. Sher Sher's parting words over the phone were, "Father, take care of yourself. Try not to worry. You will do just fine. I'll be there when you need me." Those warm, caring words, affirming support, were all he needed.

Written words expressed her feelings more than phone conversations, and so Sher Sher wrote to her father monthly, updating him about her life in the United States. She told him in her letter that he had made the right decision to bring his granddaughter out of Red China. Shau Feng could live in freedom and follow a career, thus bringing prestige and honor to the Chen women.

1

Chen Shau Feng Arrives

Lee spent almost the whole month of November waiting for some word from Pa Hu, and, when it came, he almost missed it. On November 27, exhausted from weeks of anticipation, Lee accepted an invitation to dine in a restaurant with some of his students and watch them give impromptu performances. During the course of the meal, Lee Chen became restless. After all the students had drunk a toast to him, Lee gave them all his blessing, called for the check, paid the bill, and bade them all good night.

In front of his house, as he was placing his key in the lock of the front gate, Lee sensed the presence of someone standing in the shadows nearby. Instinctively, his hand went to withdraw two knives from his belt. While flexing his left wrist, he turned to search the darkness with his eyes, but, since his night vision was not as good as it once had been, he could perceive nothing.

"Hold your hand, Master Chen! We are here, Chen Shau Feng and I have been waiting a long time for you." Pa Hu emerged from the shadows, holding a child by the hand. Lee unlocked the gate and stood inside, holding the gate open. Under the streetlight, Lee saw the child's face, which strongly resembled Sher Sher's. The same square face, stubborn chin, and unblinking eyes of Sher Sher were now looking up at him. Lee beckoned, and Pa Hu walked to the porch with Shau Feng lagging behind, carrying a small bundle in her hand. Lee ascended the porch stairs, opened the door to the house, and told them to follow him to the living room.

"Chen Shau Feng, bow to your grandfather," Pa Hu told her.

The girl obeyed silently.

"Make yourself comfortable." Lee left the room and found a large Thermos of tea and some biscuits in a box, in the kitchen. He returned to the living room and set the tray on a table and poured out tea for the three of them.

Not caring for sweets, Shau Feng sipped her tea, looked searchingly around the room, and drank in with pleasure the fragrant smell of the house. Lee decided to test the girl right away to see how well she handled herself. He thought, "I'll wager her ears are hard, which should make her very stubborn according to an old adage." He said, "Are you a Chen?" She looked him straight in the eye and nodded her head. "Are you familiar enough with our family exercise?"

"Grandfather," she replied, "I'm at your service."

Lee felt a strong surge of pride. "Only five years old and possesses such confidence," he roared. "Good! I will start, and you will continue where I leave off."

Leaving her bundle on the table, Shau Feng followed Lee out of the house and into the center of the front yard. He started the exercise, which was taught to every Chen child as soon as he or she could walk. Lee went through thirty movements with Shau Feng. The last four positions were performed incorrectly. The little girl's eyes widened as she watched her grandfather. He almost broke out laughing aloud as he recognized that familiar facial expression belonging to his late mother, Yutse.

Shau Feng said, "Grandfather, perhaps you have forgotten, but those last four positions were wrong."

Lee thought to himself, "My God, this Chen female is going to be tough and stubborn. Just look at her, locking eyes with me. At her age, I would have wet my pants before telling my grandfather that he was wrong." Aloud Lee said, "Chen Shau Feng, come, give your grandfather a hug.

Turning to the child, Pa Hu said, "Shau Feng, I'm leaving you in the care of your grandfather. Do your renowned family proud.

Good-bye, sweet child. . . . " Tears were in his eyes as he embraced Shau Feng.

"Good-bye, Uncle." Then Pa Hu said to Lee, "Master Chen, I must leave now. It isn't wise for me to be seen here. Communist spies are everywhere in Hong Kong."

"Good-bye, Pa Hu, and thank you. Give my love to all at home. Tell Agile I miss him." Lee escorted Pa Hu to the gate.

At the gate, Lee removed a heavy gold ring from his finger and pressed it into Pa Hu's hand and said, "It might be useful to you or your friends someday."

Pa Hu said, "Bless you, Master Chen. You are a good man."

After Pa Hu left, Lee led his granddaughter back into the house. She noticed that the fragrant aroma that was outside the house was also present inside. Altogether, the house was totally different from the one she was used to. Lee bombarded Shau Feng with questions.

"Child, are you hungry? Thirsty? Do you have to go to the toilet?"

"Yes, Grandfather, I want to make water." He escorted her to the bathroom, opened the door, entered and lowered the seat.

"Shau Feng, do you need my help?"

With an "I'm-not-a-baby" look, she answered, "No, I can do it by myself." In the meantime, Lee placed a rubber stopper in the bathtub drain and turned on the water, testing it to see if it was the right temperature.

"After you finish with your toilet, take a bath."

Shau Feng nodded her head. "When you finish bathing, get out of the tub, and remove the stopper. Put the stopper in the soapdish, and use these towels to dry yourself. I'll leave the pajamas and slippers, which your aunt, Sher Sher, bought you on the outside doorknob." It was late in the night when Shau Feng, exhausted, finally finished her bath.

Wearing pajamas with Disney comic animals printed on them, Shau Feng slowly entered the living room. Lee noticed the child rubbing her eyes, fighting sleep.

"Off to bed you go, Little One," said Lee. Shau Feng walked beside her grandfather, who patted her head as they went to Sher Sher's old bedroom. The old man opened the door and turned on the lights. Mrs. Kang had aired out the room so it wouldn't smell of paint.

"Into bed." Shau Feng climbed under the covers. She watched as her grandfather walked to a closet, opened the door, and reached up for something on the shelf. A broad smile spread across her face as her grandfather handed a doll to her. Shau Feng examined the doll. It had shoulder-length, curly gold hair, a pink silk dress, and open blue eyes. The doll smelled exactly the same as the house did. Thoughts were swirling around in Shau Feng's head.

"Papa acted funny when I left. He was hugging me more than he ever did before. There were tears in his eyes. During the train ride, Uncle was very strange when he spoke to me, as if I were a child. But didn't Mama say I was a big girl? Why didn't I get a reply to my question, when I asked how long I was going to be at Grandfather's house? Papa said I must be brave." Lee interrupted Shau Feng's thoughts. "Shau Feng, this is your room."

Tucking the doll under her covers, she asked, "Does the doll have a name?"

"Yes, it's Bright Star. . . . Now go to sleep. I shall turn off the light, but leave the door ajar. There will be a light left on in the hall, and the toilet door will be open." After Lee left, Shau Feng turned her head to peer at the doll.

"Do you want a hug? I would like one before I close my eyes." She fell into a sound sleep, clutching the doll to her body.

After he locked the front door, Lee brought Shau Feng's bundle from the living room to his bedroom and turned on the lights, glancing at Lavender's picture.

"Wife, the little one resembles Sher Sher." Lee opened the bundle on his desk, anxious to examine the contents.

There were Shau Feng's soiled clothes, a tiny copper Buddha

on a red string, and two envelopes. Lee stood as he opened the envelope with Shau Feng's name on it and read, "The child may possibly develop unusual talents and accomplish great things, depending on the circumstances and if the stars are in line at the time. She should not be afraid to take risks, as risks will be a major part of her life. If she is nurtured well, huge success is possible." Lee set the horoscope down and opened the letter.

Father-in-Law:
"I'm Chen Butterfly, your son Agile's wife, Shau Feng's mother, and your daughter-in-law. Thank you for accepting my child. The girl is five years old, smart, stubborn, quick of tongue, and warmhearted. If need be, I would die for my child, but it is more important that Shau Feng live. Life here is very precarious. Therefore, a mother's love will not stand in her way. Father-in-Law, I send my daughter to you for safekeeping. When we meet in the in-between life, we shall see if I owe you, or if you are repaying me. Please always reassure Shau Feng that her parents love her. Agile and I are on our knees bowing to you in deep respect and fealty."

Chen Butterfly

Lee placed the letters on his desk and went to Shau Feng's bedroom, where she was asleep, holding onto the doll. She stirred a little, and he heard her faint voice saying, "Don't worry, Mama, I will give Grandpa no trouble." Lee smiled and felt drawn to the strange but delightful child and kissed her forehead.

After Grace, his first wife, had been murdered, shot dead in their apartment in Beijing, he felt as though a part of him had died too, and he never regained his wholeness again. The horror of finding his younger son, Agile, under his mother's corpse haunted his days and nights. Loneliness and love were the prime reasons that impelled Lee to marry a young woman half his age. Lavender, with her dazzling beauty, warm heart, and clear mind, gradually filled the void in Lee's life. Her presence made him tingle all over and glad to be alive. He missed her very much. She had been his advisor, confessor, lover, and friend, and made him feel young and secure. With his daughter, Sher Sher, married and living in America, the old actor felt in limbo without a goal or real meaning to his life. As Lee peered at the sleeping child, he thanked the gods for the gift that his son and daughter-in-law had given him. He would try not to betray their trust, but would accept the responsibility.

The following morning at the breakfast table, Shau Feng was introduced to his housekeeper, Mrs. Kang, who remarked that the child resembled her aunt, Sher Sher. After the meal, Lee gave Mrs. Kang some money to have the child's hair cut and to purchase her some clothes. Lee said to Mrs. Kang, "From now on, it will be your duty to assume the care of Shau Feng, just as you did for Sher Sher. With the extra money, purchase the child some clothes and whatever else is appropriate for a five-year-old."

That afternoon, Lee left the house for Lao Mo's printing shop. Lao Mo greeted Lee warmly. The man was old and frail. He offered Lee tea, and they drank and chatted about life in general. The printer used to make fliers for the opera company and movie theaters. Recently, with a change in management in the opera company, he had lost some of his business. As a sideline, Lao Mo dealt in Black-Market documents. When Lee brought up the purpose of his visit, the man listened, nodding his head. Yes, he could help him. Lao Mo had in his possession a birth certificate of a recently deceased child whose parents were in need of money. The document was available. After a period of bargaining, they settled upon a fair price, and money changed hands.

Unhurried, Lee moved along with the crowd with the paper secured in his inside jacket pocket. Instinctively he glanced often over his shoulder. Experience had taught him that blackmailers lurked everywhere, ready to pounce upon their victims. Therefore, Lee took precautions against being followed, since Shau Feng was still an illegal alien in Hong Kong.

The next stop on his journey was to the home of a retired calligrapher who used to work for Hong Kong's Hall of Records. Mr. Mu King could alter any kind of papers and sounded pleased to be of service to Lee Chen. While Mr. King reworked the document for Chen Shau Feng, Mrs. Jade King showed Lee their art collection, which was for sale. Lee could see the rundown condition of the shop and assumed that they needed money. Pointing to the pictures, Jade said, "Local unknown artists have approached us to sell their work." Lee walked around the room, selecting a few pictures. He felt a comradeship with the young, starving artists, and so he intentionally paid more for the paintings than the asking price. It was part of Lee's generous nature to help others. After asking Mrs. King to send the paintings to his house, he left, with the altered paper once again secure in his inner jacket pocket.

During Lee's absence, Shau Feng wandered around in the big house looking into every room and closet, toting the doll under her arm wherever she went. She loved the smell of the house, and, after much questioning of Mrs. Kang, she learned that the fragrance was called lavender, which was the name of her grandfather's second wife. Shau Feng opened the refrigerator and marveled at the amount of food on the shelves, recalling that her mother had told her that food wasn't to be wasted. Shau Feng asked, "Why is there so much food in the box? Where did you get it?"

"Shau Feng, do you want something to eat?"

"No, Mrs. Kang, just looking." Seeing wonder in the child's eyes, Mrs. Kang realized she had much to do to help this child accept her new life.

In the morning of Shau Feng's third day at her grandfather's house, Prof. Yung Li Jau, a retired teacher from the Chinese-Anglo Academy, arrived. He was of medium height, had thinning white hair, wore thick, black-framed glasses, and was portly from lack of exercise. At Sher Sher's request, he was to tutor Shau Feng at her grandfather's home in all subjects, including reading, writing, and English, until she was ready to attend the Chinese-Anglo Academy. Professor Jau spoke English with a British accent, which he would pass on to Shau Feng.

It was a ritual in Chinese families to have the children's horoscopes drawn up. A week after Shau Feng's arrival, Lee sent for Wang Gwan Yee, the most famous astrologer in Hong Kong. He was a short, very soft looking, obese man who weighed over two hundred and fifty pounds. He had a round face dominated by hanging jowls and jet-black hair plastered against his scalp. To people who didn't know him, he seemed a buffoon. The most striking feature of Wang Gwan Yee was his eyes, which reflected intense power and wisdom. He was sitting on the sofa across from Lee, and Lee answered all of the questions Mr. Wang required of him.

While the men were in the living room, Mrs. Kang painstakingly prepared a large platter of tasty food as ordered by Lee. Shau Feng was outside the house playing. As fresh tea was being brewed, the aroma carried to the living room. Everything was ready to be served. Mrs. Kang waited in the kitchen for Mr. Chen to signal her to serve the refreshments. Lee coughed aloud to indicate that the negotiation was complete, and the woman carried in the huge tray. Gwan Yee's face was expressionless as Mrs. Kang set the tray on the coffee table before them and left, while Lee asked Gwan Yee to join him in the repast. Mrs. Kang stood outside the living room and watched in amazement at the rate at which the man devoured food. Her first impression of the feast was that the man had starved to death in a previous life, and was making up for it in this life.

To Gwan Yee, food inside his belly was a comfort. Its delectable taste made him smack his lips in delight. It didn't matter to him that he was fat, or that people made fun of him behind his back. He was happy. To him, being overweight was a sign of good fortune. When all the food had been consumed, the fortuneteller laboriously rocked himself to his feet. Lee stood up, and Mr. Wang said, "I'll have the chart complete in two weeks." They shook hands, and Lee showed the man out.

Two weeks later, Lee received Shau Feng's horoscope from Mr. Wang. He compared it with the one Shau Feng had brought from China. They were alike in major points. Satisfied, Lee decided to teach Shau Feng all he knew about Kung Fu. If she were to be a success, she would have to be proficient in how to defend herself in a man's world. Both charts were stored carefully in a secret compartment inside Shau Feng's bedroom closet.

Soon it was time to have dinner. Shau Feng came running into Lee's bedroom with a big smile on her face. She touched his arm.

"Grandfather, Mrs. Kang said supper is ready."

"I'm busy right now, child. You eat." From the corner of his eye, Lee noticed the girl's face change. Her head dropped, and she didn't move.

In a soft voice, Shau Feng said, "Grandfather, I don't want to eat without you. Please come eat with me." It had been a long time since Lee had had anyone depending upon him for love and emotional support. He softened, and they left the room to have dinner together. Shau Feng looked up to her grandfather. He never scolded her for running around the house or jumping on the furniture. She had plenty of clothes to wear and lots of toys to play with, and it was wonderful to learn about her ancestors. They were all Chinese Opera performers who had been famous for centuries in China. Acting, showmanship, and martial arts were in the family blood.

Beginning in January 1976, Shau Feng's days became regimented. Each morning she would practice Kung Fu under Lee's guidance. Lee made sure that she did each movement slowly and correctly. He would explain their function to her. Lee was a gentle, but a firm taskmaster. After Shau Feng exercised for the day, she took a bath and then ate breakfast with Lee. She was allowed to play before Professor Jau arrived. After the professor left, before lunch, Mrs. Kang sent her to bed for a nap. Later, she would play again until supper. From time to time, Lee allowed Shau Feng to talk to her Aunt Sher Sher over the phone.

On weekends, Lee would bring Shau Feng to the actors' workshop. There, with the other students, Shau Feng was taught how to do acrobatics, apply makeup, portray different characters, and fence and spar with the male students. Shau Feng entered the exercises eagerly and treated them as a competitive sport. The students liked her and took special care not to hurt her.

2
Fong Syang Hwa's Birthday Party

Years passed, Shau Feng was beginning to develop into a woman. Although her body had become strong and well built, she didn't like the way she looked. It seemed to her that most of her female classmates looked more feminine than she did. Their breasts were fuller, and their bodies had more curves. She would have liked her nose and ears to be different too. Chen women were late-bloomers, but there was no one around to tell her that. Lee had doubled her morning exercise period and sparred with her at home. At the performance-arts studio, when she was only allowed to perform boy's roles, Shau Feng would complain. Then her grandfather would lecture her about how to be a successful artist.

"One must be convincing in the role one portrays. An actor or actress created an illusion." In the studio, Shau Feng observed her grandfather's performance. The old man, without makeup or a costume, transformed himself into a range of characters. He not only spoke like the people represented, but took on their shapes and mannerisms. Lee's body language was a marvel to watch. Shau Feng enjoyed the physical aspect of the Chinese opera, learning how to develop agility and flexibility of her body and walking on her hands. At thirteen, Shau Feng became highly skilled in four fighting forms and obtained a "good" rating in a fifth form. This was a result of Lee's emphasis on discipline and perfect form, as well as Shau Feng's desire to please her grandfather.

Every Sunday afternoon at 3:00 P.M., Mr. Fong came to the Chen residence to play Chinese chess with Lee. Lee and Fong were long-time business partners. Sometimes, Syang Hwa, Fong's daughter and Shau Feng's classmate, accompanied him to the Chen residence to visit with her friend and take some juggling lessons.

While her grandfather inspected his late wife's potted flowers in the front yard, Shau Feng waited for Syang Hwa in the living room. Syang Hwa was five feet tall, one hundred pounds, with long, straight hair resting below her shoulders. In the neighborhood or at school, children seldom invited Shau Feng to their house to play, because their mothers feared they would be influenced by Shau Feng's ability and knowledge of Kung Fu, which they thought to be unfeminine and dangerous.

The previous week in the academy, a girl who was bigger than Syang Hwa had taken an expensive pen from her. After Shau Feng was told about it, she forced the girl to return it to Syang Hwa. Because of her physical strength and her independence, Shau Feng had become a heroine to all the girls. They looked to her for protection. When they were being bullied, a small girl at the academy used to tell the bullies who tormented them, "I'll tell Shau Feng," and then they would be left alone. Shau Feng was never afraid to take on bullies, because she knew how to fight. Sometimes she worried a little that people were treating her like a boy. Even the boys seemed to like all the other girls more than they liked her.

Syang Hwa was three months younger than Shau Feng. She invited Shau Feng to her birthday party, which was held on the first Sunday of September. This would be the first party that Shau Feng was attending where boys would be present. Shau Feng was thrilled. It was a perfect opportunity for her to meet Wing, Syang Hwa's elder brother. Every girl in the neighborhood, including Shau Feng, had a crush on the handsome youth.

Syang Hwa despised her brother, Wing. She had caught him many times pulling the wool over their mother's eyes. Wing was polite to everyone he met, yet, behind their backs, he would make fun of them to his so-called friends. The ones who "hung out" with

Wing fed the youth's weak ego. They praised everything he did or said, but in reality, Wing was a snake, a petty thief, and an accomplished liar who had a mean streak. In his mother's eyes, Wing, the handsome son, could do no wrong. On occasion, Syang Hwa found Wing in her bedroom, when there was no reason for his being there. When the young girl told Mrs. Tsi that items were missing from her bedroom, the old woman always got them back for her. When asked where she had found them, Mrs. Tsi would fix her eyes on Wing.

Lying in bed, holding Bright Star in the air by her arms, Shau Feng talked about the forthcoming party. She said to the doll, "At the party, Syang Hwa will introduce me to handsome Wing. I wonder why Syang Hwa always says bad things about her brother?" Shau Feng rose and carried Bright Star to her closet. She peered at the clothes on the hangers and thought about what she should wear for the party. To simplify the problem, she decided to copy the other girls' mode of dress. She confided in Mrs. Kang, who agreed to take her shopping to buy her some feminine-looking clothes. However, Mrs. Kang had some misgivings. She didn't believe the clothes would help all that much. Secretly she believed that Master Chen was making Shau Feng too masculine, but she would never verbalize that to the master because of her position in the household.

The night prior to Syang Hwa's birthday party, Shau Feng sat alone in her room gazing through the window at the stars in the sky for a long time. She watched the clouds altering their shape, imagining they formed a likeness of her and Wing holding hands. She fantasized that she would captivate Wing's heart and win him over all rivals. Shau Feng was filled with the emotion that her fantasies had aroused, and tears of happiness welled up in her eyes.

The day of Syang Hwa's birthday, Shau Feng arose earlier than usual and flew through her daily exercise before her running partner, Hu Hu, arrived. She went outside the front gate to wait for him.

Hu Hu, tall and wiry, was the best athlete at the performing-arts studio. They ran together every morning. Today it seemed the miles passed more quickly than ever before under Shau Fen's feet with Hu Hu trailing far behind her. Running made Shau Feng feel exhilarated. It was an escape from the tension that she sometimes felt and a way to get in touch with her body rhythm. Hu Hu called out for Shau Feng to slow down before she broke ground and soared into the air. Hu Hu, ten years senior to Shau Feng, felt the girl was too young for a serious relationship, and so he remained silent.

After the run, Shau Feng soaked in the tub and slowly and carefully washed her body with the scented soap. When she studied her nude body in the full-length mirror, she was pleased to see pubic hairs where there had been none before. Mrs. Kang entered the bedroom and found Shau Feng dressing. She studied the girl and deemed her pretty and full of youthful energy. To Mrs. Kang's question about whether she wanted something to eat, Shau Feng shook her head. The woman left the room, saying, "Have a good time."

Shau Feng waited on pins and needles until party time at 2:00 P.M. Then, carrying Syang Hwa's present, she walked out of the house. Outside in the front yard, she smiled at Mrs. Kang, who looked at her while watering her potted plants. It was a short walk from the Chen residence to where the Fongs lived. There she found the gate wide open. Shau Feng entered and was greeted by her friend, Syang Hwa, and by Mrs. Tsi, her amah. The two girls hugged each other. Syang Hwa took the present from Shau Feng and handed it to Mrs. Tsi. Following Shau Feng, more guests arrived. Mrs. Tsi told Shau Feng how good she looked. The woman liked her. Mrs. Tsi was sixtyish, but looked younger than her age; she was short, with strong arms, gray hair, and kind eyes. Mrs. Fong was busy giving orders inside the residence. Mr. Fong was nowhere in sight. Shau Feng wandered freely inside the grounds. Her heart was beating rapidly from the excitement of the day, but she greeted her friends who stopped by for a chat.

    Syang Hwa caught up with Shau Feng and took her by the arm, walking toward the rear yard, where Wing was laughing with his friends. As they approached Wing, Shau Feng turned her head away to hide her blushing cheeks.

    Wing's good looks made him stand out in a crowd. The young man was impeccably dressed. He was tall, of medium build, his handsome face dominated by a prominent nose and long eyelashes. To Shau Feng, Wing was a vision of manliness. He was wearing a powder-blue suit that had been especially tailored for the party, and he wore embellishments of golden jewelry like his father. Gathered around him were young men who talked and laughed aloud to attract girls' attention. A youth with pimples on his face served as a lookout for Wing. When he saw Syang Hwa coming with Shau Feng, he signaled Wing with a wink and roll of his eyes. Wing was exhilarated. Now was the time to avenge Syang Hwa's insult, which had made him lose face before his friends. Syang Hwa had openly dared to say that Shau Feng's fighting skill was superior to his, which made her Syang Hwa's protector. That was the last straw; Wing couldn't take that from his sister, who looked down on him and looked up to Shau Feng.

    Syang Hwa was aware that Wing's friends praised him for his natural fighting ability. They allowed him to best them in a mock fight to satisfy his ego. Wing was an admirer of his own good looks and believed others should share the same admiration and show him respect. Today he would carry out his plot to insult Shau Feng, smack her face, and send her home in tears. Then Syang Hwa would get the message as to who was the superior fighter.

    When Wing saw Shau Feng coming his way with his sister, he deliberately turned his back on them. He turned to his friends and said, "Do you know my stupid sister invited that wildcat Shau Feng to this party? That simpleminded girl must be hard up for presents. My mother said many times that Master Chen found Shau Feng in the gutter and brought her home." The youths around Wing snickered. "Also, do you know that old Chen raped a girl half his age? Her poor parents wanted to take him to court, but that sly old devil used his money to pay them off and get a young wife in the bargain. To this day, my parents don't believe Mr. Chen fathered his daughter, Sher Sher." Shau Feng, at the beginning, only heard Wing's voice, not quite catching the meaning of the words. When she finally comprehended what was being said, the smile vanished from her face, her heart sank, and fire showed in her eyes. A sharp involuntary yell came from Shau Feng as she advanced toward Wing. He heard it, but paid no attention to her as the crowd backed away from him. Wing turned to face Shau Feng with an innocent smile on his arrogant face.

Shau Feng shouted, "Those are stupid lies, you loudmouth clown!"

His eyes caught his sister's. A sinister expression appeared on his face. Shau Feng's outburst gave him provocation. Quickly he moved his hand from his side to slap Shau Feng's face, but he wasn't as fast as she. Her blow stung his face. Wing suddenly pulled his head back, reaching for his stinging red cheek. In disbelief, he said, "The bitch hit me!" An angry Shau Feng looked daggers at Wing.

"You dirty dog, you're a real rotter...." Wing was humiliated by having been slapped in front of his friends. He attacked her with his fists. It seemed to onlookers that Shau Feng had effortlessly brushed away Wing's fists. This was countered by her punches that landed against Wing's midsection, doubling him over. Looking at her in amazement, feeling the pain from her blows, he wanted to cry. With the insults to her family ringing in her ears, an enraged Shau Feng vigorously slapped Wing's face again and again, rocking his head with each contact. None dared to stop Shau Feng.

Shouts and female screams above the din brought Mr. Fong to the rear garden. Shocked by what he saw, he hurried to step between Shau Feng and his son, preventing her from striking Wing's swollen face. Angered by the scene, Mr. Fong ordered Shau

Feng to leave the party. She turned on her heels and walked away. He called, "Miss Chen, I will talk with your grandfather about this episode."

Emerging from the house, hearing of the fight in the rear garden, Mrs. Fong went to see what had occurred. Horrified at the sight of Wing's battered face, her facial expressions went from being stunned to white-hot rage. She went to comfort her son. Mrs. Fong's red eyes peered at the youths' faces in the crowd as she loudly demanded, "Who did this to my son?"

A whimpering Wing replied, "It was Shau Feng, mama." The irate woman looked for Shau Feng among the crowd, but, by then, she was gone. A vexed Syang Hwa tried to get her parents' attention, but neither one would listen. She thought that her bastard of a brother had gotten what he deserved. Mrs. Fong cradled her son in her arms, aching over his swollen cheeks and puffed eyes. In her mind, nobody but a monster would harm her darling child.

Shau Feng was furious as she walked rapidly home. "How dare Wing tell lies and insult my family in public! Did he think I would let him get away with it? That bloody bastard!" She slammed the gate shut and entered the house, stomping into her bedroom. Inside the room, Shau Feng looked for something to throw. Suddenly the girl felt warm fluid running down her leg. She looked at the pool of blood dripping on the floor and covering her sneaker. She shouted, "Oh, God, my life's blood is flowing out of me. What has happened to me?"

Mrs. Kang heard the shout and came into Shau Feng's bedroom. She saw Shau Feng standing and staring at the blood on the floor. She said carefully and distinctly, "Shau Feng, you are having your monthly period. Calm yourself and take off your bloody clothes and sneakers. I'll come with some water for you to wash yourself." Returning with water and a towel, she handed Shau Feng a sanitary napkin and patted her on the head, saying, "It's nothing to worry about; it's something that will occur every month. You are now a woman and can have children. Go to your room, change your clothes, and rest a while." With her temper at its highest, the news that she was a woman didn't appease her. Shang Hwa was right. Her eyes were open. Wing was no good.

Carrying several new suits he had bought that afternoon, Lee returned home. The suits were hung in his closet, and he made himself a drink. Lee went outside to inspect Lavender's potted plants. When he saw that they had been watered, he was satisfied. He walked to the porch and sat in his favorite chair to await Shau Feng's return. It was a pleasantly warm day, and he closed his eyes and reflected about the recent events. Lee's thoughts were interrupted by the harsh sounds of a woman's voice berating someone. He opened his eyes as the noise grew louder. Mr. Fong, with his entire family behind him, appeared at the front gate. He leaned on the bell. Lee let them in. They entered the yard without greeting him. The 5'6", 170-pound Mrs. Fong had a ruddy face, which, though still as pretty as when she was young, at the moment was so filled with hate that she appeared ugly. Syang Hwa looked at her brother as if she wanted to hit him.

Mr. Fong shouted at Lee Chen, "Our friendship ends today, if you don't do something about Shau Feng's atrocious behavior!" Syang Hwa tried to speak, but her father wasn't in any mood to listen to her. Hearing the loud voices, Shau Feng stuck her head out of the window, calling to her grandfather. Lee Chen calmly asked everyone to wait while he talked to his granddaughter.

Mrs. Fong, yelled, "No, that won't do! I'll go up and get her myself!"

"I'm the master of this house, not you! You will wait here. Otherwise, leave my house now! Do I make myself clear, Mrs. Fong?"

Lee's intimidating, icy voice caused the woman to stop in her tracks. She glanced at her husband for support. Mr. Fong was silent. This was a side of Mr. Chen he had never seen before. With his head held high, Lee entered the house, went to Shau Feng's room, and knocked on the door. He saw a fuming Chen woman holding her doll, standing at the window. She appeared ready for a fight. Gently he said, "Young Chen, come with me. The Fongs are here."

Outside, Shau Feng followed her grandfather to the porch and stood with her back against a post. Lee walked to where a thin, six-foot bamboo pole lay on the ground. He picked it up and swung it through the air. The sound the pole made, moving through the air, riveted the Fongs' attention. Master Chen approached Shau Feng. He stopped several feet away, raising the pole high over his head. Swiftly it came down, striking the porch post, inches over her head. Shau Feng didn't flinch. Wing's swollen face paled. He tightly held onto his mother's arm. Syang Hwa and Mr. Fong cringed. The girl's mouth was open, yet she couldn't make a sound. Syang Hwa wanted to run to her friend, but her feet were rooted to the ground. Shau Feng's anger subsided. She realized her grandfather was putting on a show for the Fongs. Lee's second strike stopped inches from Shau Feng's face.

Mr. Fong cried, "Master Chen, she is still a child! You could kill her!" Lee dramatically threw the pole to the ground. He ignored Mr. Fong.

"Shau Feng, the Chens tell the truth, no matter what happens. Now please act like a Chen." In came the girl's stubborn chin, and her fists were clenched. Shau Feng related her side of the story. Lee saw that Syang Hwa nodded her head in agreement with Shau Feng's tale. He noticed that Wing was trembling, and Mr. Fong showed shock on his face as he stared at his son. Mrs. Fong still had her protective arms around her son. A much-subdued Mr. Fong asked his son to tell his side of the story. The whimpering youth looked at his mother for support.

Mrs. Fong said, "Wing, my son, don't be afraid. Mama is here."

Looking straight into his mother's face, Wing said, "Shau Feng beat me because I told her jokingly that I was fond of another girl who was prettier than her. You know how wild she can be. I tried to calm her, but she started to hit me. I couldn't strike her back, because it is unmanly." Mr. Fong hung his head. He was unable to look directly at Lee.

Mrs. Kang, who was listening from the open kitchen window, was furious. She muttered, "I would have done more to the snake in the grass than slap his face." Lee cleared his throat, and the Fongs' eyes went to him.

He said, "Shau Feng, apologize to Mr. and Mrs. Fong for hitting their son." Shau Feng bowed to her grandfather without arguing. Facing the Fongs, she apologized. The old actor's voice was ice cold. "Young lady, for your action at the Fong residence, from today on, you are never to associate with them. Now go to your room!" Syang Hwa found her voice.

"Master Chen, it's unfair to punish Shau Feng when she told the truth. I was there. What she did was to defend her family's name. Oh, please . . . " She began to cry.

Mr. Fong realized he was caught between Wing's lie and his wife's berating. He mumbled to Lee, "Master Chen, you are too severe with Shau Feng." Lee raised his hand to stop him from saying more.

"Mr. Fong, you and your family are no longer welcome in my house. Children echo what they hear from their parents. Leave this very minute!" Mr. Chen went to the gate and opened it wide. Mrs. Fong's face registered disappointment. In her way of thinking, Shau Feng was the guilty one. Mr. Fong was in shock. He refused to believe thirty years of friendship had been brought to an end by his son's stupidity. The Fongs left, and Lee slammed the gate shut behind them.

Mrs. Kang intercepted Lee on his way to the living room. The woman was in a state of agitation. She said, "Master Chen, it's obvious that Wing Fong lied. Shau Feng is not the wildcat people call her. She is good and kindhearted; besides, she never tells lies."

The aged actor touched her shoulder to silence her. Sadness appeared on his face. "Yes, I know Shau Feng told the truth, and Wing lied. Nevertheless, the girl must learn she can't stop malicious gossip with her fists. Gossip is the cheapest form of entertainment at the expense of others without feeling responsible for the action."

"That is right, sir. To stop the mouths of people is more difficult than to deal with a river in flood. Master Chen, I have something to tell you, sir. Today, there is no longer a child in your house. Shau Feng is now a woman. Do you comprehend what I'm trying to tell you?"

"A woman . . . ?" Lee looked puzzled. Mrs. Kang nodded her head.

"Yes, sir, Shau Feng is a woman." The old actor went to the bar and poured out two brandies. One, he gave to Mrs. Kang.

"To womanhood, Mrs. Kang." They drank to that toast. Lee said, "Mrs. Kang, I shall not need you until Monday. You may go home to your family now. Shau Feng and I will dine out."

Lee knocked on Shau Feng's door and asked permission to enter.

"Granddaughter, I heard the most wonderful news today. Is it true, that you have now entered into womanhood?" Shau Feng nodded her head.

"At first, Grandpa, I was very frightened and thought I had ruptured a blood vessel."

He shook his head, "No, my child, you have been given the gift given to every woman, the gift that is the most feminine part of her, the ability to be a mother and have children. Through you, Shau Feng, someday I might be a great-grandfather." He took her in his arms, and they hugged for a while.

"How do you know all this about women, Grandfather?"

"I was well taught by your beautiful grandmother. She would be very proud of you today—as I am." He kissed her cheek and gently shut the door behind him.

The actor entered his bedroom and gazed longingly at his wife's picture. With a face showing unhappiness, Lee said, "Wife, much joy and some unhappiness. Today Shau Feng became a woman. I hope some of your loveliness will grow on her. Also, it isn't easy at my age to throw away friends. Most of them usually leave you by dying. Today's incident made me lose a friend of thirty years. Tonight Shau Feng and I dine out. Afterwards, I shall buy her a pair of jade earrings, as beautiful as yours that now belong to Sher Sher. There are times like these, I feel I have lived too long. How I long for you. How I regret your not being here to comfort me in my old age."

Syang Hwa was filled with wretchedness from the loss of her dearest friend. She glared daggers at her treacherous brother. Her young heart was consumed with enmity. Away from the Chen residence, Wing felt courageous enough to give his sister a wolfish grin as they entered their yard. That look triggered an explosion inside the girl. Syang Hwa looked around to find something with which to hit her brother. There on the ground were the handles of several croquet mallets. With determination and force she had never before experienced, the girl picked up a wooden handle and started to attack her brother. Syang Hwa's first blow struck Wing's back. He turned, raising an arm to protect himself. Syang Hwa beat at his arms and legs with a will. Wing howled from pain and fell to the ground. Mrs. Fong screamed at Syang Hwa and tried to stop her.

Mr. Fong held his wife back, saying, "The boy is spoiled! He deserves everything he is getting. Why are you so blind?"

Finally he restrained Syang Hwa, who shrieked, "Animal, if I ever hear you lie about Shau Feng again, I'll cripple you. She is worth a hundred of you!"

Syang Hwa ran to her room. The housekeeper was in the room straightening out the drawers. When she saw Syang Hwa crying bitterly, Mrs. Tsi opened her arms, and Syang Hwa ran into them. Her entire body shook as she sobbed, "Shau Feng is lost to me because Wing lied. Because of this incident, life will never be the same. Telling lies seems to be easier for some than telling the truth."

Mrs. Tsi thought before replying, "Telling the truth is easy if you are strong enough to bear the consequences—which sometimes can be very unpleasant."

3
Graduation

It was the graduation day, June, 1986, at the Chinese-Anglo Academy for Girls. All, with the exception of Shau Feng, wore big smiles on their faces. Her last year at the academy had not been a happy one. From the start, Shau Feng had been informed by her grandfather that a transcript of her school records was being sent to Plainfield College, in Ohio, in America.

On this day, wealthy families packed the exclusive school grounds. They walked about the exercise field that served as a reception area. The weather was warm, with the hot sun overhead. The academy instructors and administrators mingled with the graduates and their families. Behind the refreshment stand, a band was playing music. Young women pointed Shau Feng and her grandfather out to their parents. Some parents came over to meet Mr. Chen. They were flattered by his presence. Lee even consented to have his picture taken with some of them. The retired actor was a very familiar face to the general public. Shau Feng stood beside her grandfather, holding six yellow roses in her hand. Suddenly Shau Feng felt someone touch her back. She turned around to find Syang Hwa. Quickly Syang Hwa threw her arms around Shau Feng's neck and passed a small package to her friend. Syang Hwa hugged Shau Feng again and went away in tears. Shau Feng bit her lip. She looked at her grandfather and put the package inside her pocket. Shau Feng looked at Syang Hwa from a distance and waved at her. It was all she could do to prevent herself from openly crying.

Later Lee greeted an administrator who thanked him for his

daughter's generous gift to the academy and reassured Lee that Shau Feng's records were being processed by Plainfield College, in Ohio, in the U.S.A. Lee glanced at Shau Feng, whose eyes were downcast. He patted the top of her head, and she looked up at him dolefully. The actor, who was wearing a smile, said, "Smile, Chen Donkey. The world has not come to an end. Remember, you come from an acting family, so act happy." Lee peered at the faces in the crowd. He saw Mr. Fong looking directly at him. Mr. Fong bowed to Lee, who returned the same gesture.

After the graduation ceremony had concluded, Lee asked Shau Feng if there were anyone else to whom she wished to say good-bye. She shook her head, and they walked out of the academy compound to their rented limo, which would bring them to a restaurant. Lee reminded Shau Feng that she was to travel in the morning from Hong Kong, via Japan, to Los Angeles. There, her Aunt Sher Sher and Uncle Charles would meet her at the L.A. International Airport. She nodded her head. Lee said, "At least you had your donkey ears open when your Aunt Sher Sher was talking to you last night over the phone."

After dinner, they went straight home, because Shau Feng was to catch the first flight to America. The young woman went directly to her bedroom to finish packing her clothes. Master Chen headed for the living room. Lee thought about what he wished to tell Shau Feng. It was time for her to understand what she would face in America. The old master poured himself a drink.

Meanwhile Shau Feng, in her bedroom, took out the package Syang Hwa had given her and opened it. There was a note inside. She read,

> I never had the opportunity to express my thanks for all the kindnesses and love you have shown me over the years. I thought our friendship would last forever. It had been my wish that one of your children would marry one of mine. That would make us related. That wonderful dream was abruptly shattered because of Wing's

evil action. I despair at your leaving Hong Kong. I sense I might never see you again. Did you know that I had taken many pictures of you at the academy? I keep them all in my album. The good ones as well as the ones that didn't come out so well. I shall never forget you.

Love,
Fong Syang Hwa

Shau Feng set the note on her bed and opened the box. It contained a gold pin resembling a flower. On the back of the pin was engraved, "Friendship Forever." Shau Feng made a mental note to call Syang Hwa from Japan, since she was leaving early the next morning, and now it was too late. There wouldn't be time to visit or call from home. Shau Feng stamped her foot from frustration. She was determined to speak once more to her grandfather about remaining in Hong Kong.

She confronted him in the living room. As she dropped to her knees in front of him, her forehead touched the carpet. Lee let out a great sigh, "Young Chen, get your head off my carpet, and please listen to me. I'm sending you to America, because I want the very best for you. I want you to be the most you can be. Please give serious consideration to becoming a lawyer. That profession will open many doors for you—political science, teaching, community service, and the like. Now give me a nice smile. Don't give your aunt and uncle any trouble. Study hard to make a name for the Chens and our fellow Chinese. Above all, young lady, be proud to be Chinese and try to accept the Americans, even if some of them act crazy." Shau Feng broke into a smile, but hid her face from her grandfather. "Come sit by me and listen to what I have to tell you. Your Uncle Charles prefers male children. Use your acting ability to behave like a male. I'm sure once he gets to know you, he will love you as much as I do."

Lee arose to hug her, and she responded with open arms, saying, "I'll prove to Uncle Charles that girls are just as good as boys, maybe even better." They both broke into a laugh and tightly hugged each other.

Alone in the living room, Lee forced himself not to think how letting go of Shau Feng would affect his life. Like Shau Feng's parents, he couldn't bring himself to hinder Shau Feng's future. A feeling of depression settled over Lee like a heavy mist. He lamented, "Oh, how the years pass so slowly for the young and fly on the wings of eagles for the old. It seems like yesterday, the child was dragging her doll around the house. Now she is a grown woman on the road to college." Lee swelled with pride, visualizing his granddaughter.

"That child can be hot one moment and cool the next, but Chen women can't remain angry for long. It isn't in their nature. They are truly compassionate individuals." Lee tried to recall Sher Sher, the way his daughter looked, strong, beautiful and intelligent. With that thought of beauty in mind, the old master reentered the distant past, and daydreams once more brought Lavender to life. He fell asleep dreaming Lavender was in his arms.

On the last night in her grandfather's house, Shau Feng was restless. She couldn't sleep for thinking about leaving her grandfather and his lavender-scented house. It had been her home for almost thirteen, very happy years. The six yellow roses her grandfather gave her represented the inner self of Chen women. It was part of the family tradition for an important occasion. Shau Feng placed the yellow roses under the picture of Mrs. Lavender Chen and thanked her grandmother for having allowed her to dwell in her house in peace. But, intuitively, she knew she could not stop time. She closed her eyes, and the lavender scent calmed and refreshed her spirit. Her mind wandered back to a time when she had gone to a church service with a school chum. Most of the ceremony had been foreign to her, but she remembered the message of the minister. He was talking about accepting change, and he repeated a quote that he said came from the Old Testament of the Bible: "'To everything there is a season and a time for everything.'"

She also remembered giggling at the time, thinking that the words sounded familiar, as if they might have been something Confucius had said.

But now she realized the truth of the words. It was time to grow up and leave the warm, comfortable, cared-for childhood. Clutching her doll, she kissed it and said, "Good-bye, my darling. It is time to go. I love you very much. You've always been a great comfort to me. I'll remember you forever." She lay down, curled up with the doll, just as she had lain down for many years, and finally she fell asleep. If anyone had looked in on that scene, he surely would have thought that both were smiling. Shau Feng's future had begun!

4

America and Ohio

At the Los Angeles International Airport, Shau Feng left the immigration section and went to the customs inspection station, dragging two pieces of luggage. A young Chinese customs inspector took the form from Shau Feng and read "Miss Shau Feng Chen, from Hong Kong." He asked, "Anything to declare, miss? I see you are going to Ohio." She shook her head in reply. The young man stamped the declaration form and handed it back with a wink.

"Have a good trip to Ohio, Miss Chen." Color came to her face, as she looked back at the young man. His wink made her feel strangely uncomfortable.

Outside, the exit was jammed with people waiting. Shau Feng gazed at the crowd, searching for the huge form of her American Uncle Charles. She couldn't locate either her uncle or her aunt. A porter came over and asked if she needed assistance.

"No," she said. Recalling her grandfather's instructions about her behavior and appearance, and that she was to act more masculine to win Uncle Charles's affection, she put on her Greek fisherman's cap and closed her jacket up to the neck. Shau Feng then sat, straddling her luggage, and waited.

Five miles from the L.A. International Airport, Sher Sher and Charles, in a limousine, were held up in heavy traffic on the freeway because there had been an accident. It was long past Shau Feng's arrival time, and so Charles, using a mobile phone, called the airline customer service. The agent informed him that the flight from Hong Kong, via Japan to L.A., had been on the ground for thirty minutes.

Finally, an hour later, they arrived at the Los Angeles International Airport Arrivals Building and hurriedly pushed through the doors, heading straight for the arrivals waiting area. The place was a beehive of activity with faces and bodies of all races and descriptions milling about. Sher Sher removed Shau Feng's picture from her pocketbook and looked at it for the third time that day. She had become anxious, because they were already over an hour late. Charles, usually a calm person, was beginning to get testy. For a moment Sher Sher's eyes rested on a Chinese youth wearing a lumber jacket and Greek fisherman's cap. Then she looked away and continued her search in the crowd. For some reason, she redirected her attention to the Chinese youth and pondered for a moment.

"That boy looks like me," she said and then called out loud in Chinese, "Chen Shau Feng, where are you?"

"I'm here!" Up went Shau Feng's arm in the air as she stood. Charles, with Sher Sher behind him, tried to force their way through the crowd that seemed bent on impeding their progress.

But Charles, with his six-foot-six frame and two hundred sixty pounds of muscle, won out, and he finally beat a path to where Shau Feng was standing. Charles looked at Shau Feng and with a smile asked himself, "Don't young women dress like females any more?" Shau Feng grinned back at him, and they embraced warmly.

On the other hand, Sher Sher was shocked at Shau Feng's appearance. She yanked the cap off her head and said in her high-pitched voice, "Well, young man—or young woman—let's have a look at you." Shau Feng did a little pirouette in front of her aunt and uncle. They all laughed and hugged each other with Chinese and English flowing back and forth.

Charles finally broke it up, saying, "Ladies, follow me." Effortlessly, he lifted the suitcases and shepherded his wife and niece through the crowd to the exit. When the Lemars came out of the door, the limo driver ushered them to the waiting car, where they were finally ensconced with Shau Feng.

Sandwiched between her uncle and aunt in the back seat of the limo, Sher Sher finally broke the silence.

"Today is a complete disaster. First, the hotel elevators were down; second, there was the accident on the freeway; and third, Shau Feng arrived, looking like God-knows-what." Sher Sher turned to Shau Feng and said in rapid Chinese, "Why aren't you dressed properly? What kind of costume is that?" Sher Sher's words were critical, but her voice was kind—and Shau Feng responded obediently.

"Grandfather told me Uncle Charles only likes male children! He said that I must make a boyish impression on my American uncle." The young woman's statement was like a pin puncturing a balloon. The anger quickly subsided, and a burst of laughter came out of Sher Sher.

"Father told you that?" Shau Feng nodded her head. "Where did he ever get that silly notion?" Sher Sher pulled Shau Feng closer to her. She thought, "Oh, God, it seems Father misunderstood what I told him years ago. Now my white lies have come back to haunt me. Just look at her! Doesn't she look exactly like me, but younger and stronger? She even smells of lavender." Charles was silent in the car, because the two women's Chinese was too fast for him to catch what was being said. He knew they both could speak flawless English, and he felt left out of the conversation.

In the luxury hotel, Shau Feng's room adjoined her aunt's and uncle's. The Lemars had arrived in L.A. the day before from Ohio, to be on hand to meet Shau Feng at the airport. Back in the room, Charles was on the phone, confirming their next-morning flight back to Cincinnati, Ohio. Sher Sher wanted to see how her niece was doing. She entered Shau Feng's room to see Shau Feng standing by the window, looking at the street below. By Sher Sher's standards, Shau Feng's clothes looked awful. They weren't suitable for a young lady entering college. But now was not the right moment to voice displeasure. Shau Feng turned to see her aunt looking at her. In a moment, they both opened their arms wide and embraced each other.

Shau Feng began to cry. It took Sher Sher by surprise.

"Why are you sobbing?"

"I miss Grandfather. I have lived with him for thirteen years."

Charles came into Shau Feng's room through the open door. He saw the young woman in tears and asked, "Are you all right?" Sher Sher nodded her head and gestured to Charles to leave the room. After he went out the door, Sher Sher cuddled Shau Feng in her arms again.

"Stop crying, Shau Feng. You will give your American uncle the wrong impression. Remember, the entire Chen clan is lion-hearted—even the women. We were born tough women." Shau Feng raised her head to face Sher Sher.

Suddenly, a memory materialized in Sher Sher's mind. There she was as a young child, mourning over her dead mother's body in a coffin. She was pleading with her mother to rise and come home. There were other people in the room standing behind her. They were saying, "It's a pity, such a beautiful woman, with everything to live for, had to die so young. It's a shame that her little daughter is motherless." As the scene faded from her mind, she found herself kissing Shau Feng, who was clutching Sher Sher tightly. They had a moment of togetherness and love.

Laughing nervously, Sher Sher touched Shau Feng's face, saying, "Darling, would you like to freshen up before dinner?"

"Yes, please, Auntie." Her eyes were shining.

Charles was watching a Western movie on TV merely to kill time. When Sher Sher returned, he studied his wife's face carefully and was relieved to see it reflected lightheartedness, good cheer, and happiness. Sher Sher said, "Charles, let's have a mini-vacation instead of flying home tomorrow. Mr. Ko can handle the business end of the negotiations with the Taiwan group." Charles was taken back. This was so uncharacteristic of Sher Sher. She never allowed anyone to handle a million-dollar contract without being present. However, the idea of a vacation was tempting.

"Great idea, kid. I'll reschedule our flight for Sunday. That will give us more than five days to enjoy California."

"Wonderful, Darling."

The big man studied his wife. Gone were the hard lines from around her mouth, and her eyes sparkled as they had in their honeymoon days. She was humming a Chinese song that he hadn't heard her sing in years. Mentally, he roared, "Welcome to America, Shau Feng. You should have come years ago."

5
In Ohio

It was 6:00 A.M., on the first day of Shau Feng's arrival at the Lemar House, in Ohio. She stepped out the front door into the sunshine. A golden retriever was on the lawn, playing with a ball. The Lemars had bought the dog five years before, after their first dog, Dede, had died. Sher Sher had named the Golden Retriever "Shau De." When Shau Feng came out to the lawn, the dog ran over, checking her out, smelling her up and down. One sniff told him that this new person was possibly a friend. Shau Feng rubbed the dog's head and spoke to him gently. A wagging tail was his welcoming response.

Feeling the need of physical activity, Shau Feng went through her Kung Fu sequences. She ran around the estate with the dog barking at her heels. The geese on the rear grounds of the estate woke up and joined in the fun, flapping their wings and honking when Shau Feng and Shau De ran past the pond. The place was electrified with comradeship and happy fun.

Exhausted, Shau Feng finally dropped on the lawn to rest and to study the exterior of the house. It was a rectangular, two-story, red-brick house, with a black-tile roof, and dual chimneys. The downstairs windows were larger than the top-floor ones. Two huge front doors were painted red, with brass knobs shining in the sunlight. There was a four-car garage off to the side of the circular driveway. In the center of the lawn was a fountain of stone fish and birds throwing water into the air from their open mouths. Turning on her side, Shau Feng spotted a double road that led from the house to the two wrought-iron decorative gates. A ten-foot gray-brick wall encircled the entire estate. Around the walls on the inside were thick evergreen hedges, which grew close together, forming a beautiful green boundary.

One evening, Sher Sher took Shau Feng into town to shop for an entire new wardrobe. Shau Feng was encouraged by Sher Sher to discard the clothes she had brought with her from Hong Kong. Shau Feng didn't care for the idea of wasting good clothes, but Sher Sher laughed and said, "It's all right, Dear. It's only money."

"Auntie, isn't money important? Shouldn't we try to save it? Some people don't have any at all." Over supper, the women settled upon a truce. They would keep the clothes until they decided what to do with them. After eating, the women walked arm in arm browsing through the downtown streets while they shared some of the high points of their life stories.

Rain or shine, each morning, Shau Feng went through her exercise routine, which included running one or two miles. One Saturday morning, she was in the backyard playing with the dog, when Charles emerged from the house carrying a football. He was impressed when he saw Shau Feng perform a series of cartwheels, backflips and handstands. He shouted to her, "Heads up, Shau Feng!" He tossed the ball in her direction. To his surprise, she easily caught the football. Pleased, they spent the rest of the morning tossing the football between them. Charles watched as Shau Feng covered the ground quickly to get to the ball. She reminded him of himself, when in his youth he always followed the ball's movement in the air. The dog, Shau De, joined in the fun, romping back and forth, barking and trying to catch the ball. Charles thought to himself, "If Shau Feng were a boy, she would make a great player. Should I encourage her to try out for sports? Maybe I'd better check it out with Sher Sher, since she's so anxious to make Shau Feng into a young lady." Sher Sher was observing her husband and Shau Feng hurling the football between them with the dog jumping to get the ball, and was having some private thoughts of her own.

That afternoon, Shau Feng accompanied Charles to town to pick up some custom-made shirts he had ordered from the haberdasher. Shau Feng's new dresses were also ready, and so Charles showed Shau Feng the direction to walk to the ladies shop, and he said he would meet her there later. Shau Feng was wearing blue jeans, a fisherman's cap on her head, gold earrings on her earlobes, and bright red polish on her nails. A freshly washed face, with no makeup, completed the picture.

Gary's Pizza Parlor was on Hausen Ave. It was a hangout for idle youths to kill time. Across the street from the pizza parlor was Rush's Coffee Shop. There sat two policemen, sipping their coffee. Shau Feng was working her way toward the pizza parlor to buy a Coke on the way to the dress store. As she came within ten feet of the parlor, a short, slender youth came out of the parlor to block her way. He was looking for excitement. His entire week had been dull. He shouted at his buddies, "Hey, fellahs, look what we have here—a drag queen." The youth, encouraged by the presence of his chums, said to Shau Feng, "Hello, Chink faggot, your ass is mine!" This made everyone laugh, which encouraged him. The youth wanted to do something to draw the girls' attention to him—to show them that he was macho, not a short punk. Shau Feng didn't understand the boy's strange words, but sensed from his menacing tone that his intention was not good. The boy extended his arms to shove Shau Feng off the sidewalk. Surprisingly, he found himself being spun around and tossed into the gutter. The youth landed on his rear. Getting to his feet, he discovered his pants were torn at his behind.

The girls outside the pizza parlor were roaring with laughter. He became furious. He couldn't stand being ridiculed. "Motherfucker," he shouted, as his face turned scarlet. He attacked Shau Feng again with his fists flying. Shau Feng blocked his punches and struck his chest with her elbow. Backward went the youth a few steps, as he stopped to rub his hurt chest. When his friends came to his aid, they too received punches and kicks, just as the policemen piled out of Rush's Diner to deal with the fracas.

Sergeant Swab said to his companion, "Doesn't that Chinese youth come from the Lemar estate?"

"That looks like the kid who plays with their dog."

"The Lemars must be in town. Better bring the kid to them before things get out of hand." The younger policeman asked Shau Feng if she were there alone. When she said her uncle was in the haberdashery, the policeman escorted her there. The older cop then went over to restrain the hostile youths. An idea was forming in his brain.

"I'll use this occasion to teach those punks a lesson." Calling Shau Feng by the name "Hoy Lee," he said, "Little Joe, how would you and young Hoy Lee like to finish the fight at the P.A.L.?" Little Joe backed into the crowd. He couldn't look the policeman in the eye. "Is that a no?" The policeman intimidated the youths. "Listen, I don't want any of you to cause trouble for the rest of the summer; otherwise I'll invite Hoy Lee over to give you some lessons in the manly art of self-defense. Now behave yourselves."

The younger policeman came back and stood behind his partner. He said in a low voice, "I brought the Chinese kid to Goldman's store. I saw Charles Lemar inside, but I didn't mention anything to him about a fight."

"Good." The boys and girls started to walk away from the pizza parlor. Sergeant Swab said, "Now tell me if the kid is a queer or a girl?"

"I don't know."

"Did you ever see anyone who could fight that well against a crowd?"

"Sure, but only in the movies."

During that scuffle, some shoppers and store workers had stopped to watch the commotion. It added some excitement to an otherwise dull day. Mrs. Jay Lawson, a jeweler's wife, was among the crowd. She recognized the Chinese youth as the one she had seen with Mrs. Lemar three days before. Jay couldn't imagine why the boys had picked on a girl. When the fight was over, Mrs. Lawson walked rapidly back to her husband's store. She went straight into the small office in the back of the shop. There she dialed Mrs. Lemar's telephone number, after looking it up in the phone book. She could hardly contain the excitement and admiration in her voice, as she recounted the story to Mrs. Lemar over the phone.

During the ride back home, Charles observed Shau Feng from the corner of his eye, because she was very quiet and had no packages. He asked, "I thought your dresses were ready." Shau Feng didn't say a word. He saw her chin was pulled in like Sher Sher's, when she was angry. He said, "Hey, Little Phoenix, cat got your tongue? I asked you if the dresses were ready?"

The words flew out of her mouth, relating the fight with some boys. Then she paused to inquire, "Uncle, what is a drag queen? And what is a faggot?"

"Where did you hear that kind of talk?" Charles glanced again at the girl. Shau Feng's mouth was compressed to a straight, thin line. The big man knew from that expression that he wouldn't get an answer until he explained the slang word. He told her that it was a derogatory expression for a man who acts like a woman, a homosexual, who although he had a man's body, mentally felt feminine. Shau Feng was confused, but she understood enough to know that Little Joe had been making fun of her because he thought she was a homosexual. She felt angry and sad that there were people in the world who made fun of other people because they were different. She asked Charles to take her back to the restaurant. She promised not to attack the youths. She just wanted to convince them how wrong their thinking was. Charles refused, saying they had better drop the whole thing, because they couldn't save the world. There would be plenty of time ahead for that.

"Shau Feng, don't mention the fight to your aunt. It would be better for both of us if she didn't know about it."

"Okay, it's forgotten," she agreed, knowing that Sher Sher would be upset, since a softer image was what she wanted for Shau Feng.

A fuming Sher Sher waited outside the house. The big gray sedan came to a stop by the garage. Charles got out and waved to his wife. By the look on her face, Charles knew that Sher Sher had learned of the fight.

"Charles, how could you let her get into a fight with those boys? She could have gotten hurt!"

"Those jerks picked on the wrong person today."

Sher Sher's voice went several octaves higher. "Shau Feng is supposed to be a well-mannered young woman, not a barroom brawler!"

With Shau Feng behind him, Charles walked toward Sher Sher and stood his ground. "Hold your horses, old girl, I remember the time I took you to a Tex-Mex restaurant, where two toughs wanted to see if I was as rough off the field as on it."

Stamping her foot on the porch, she replied, "It's not the same situation!" Charles placed his hands on his hips, and said, "Who kicked the guys in the groin? Who punched out their lights?" A sharp edge came to Sher Sher's voice. She didn't want to be reminded of those days.

"I didn't knock them cold; you did! This is different. Do you hear me? All Chen women are strong, but they are also feminine. Is that so hard for you to understand!"

Sher Sher examined Shau Feng from head to toe. When she was certain nothing was wrong with the girl, she ordered, "Shau Feng, go to your room. Charles will be up shortly to talk to you." Feeling resentful and misunderstood, Shau Feng walked heavily into the house, slamming the front door shut. Sher Sher aimed a reproving eye at her husband.

"You will rebuke Shau Feng, remind her to be better behaved."

Charles knew better than to argue with his wife when she was angry. As he walked into the house, he muttered, "What is wrong with Sher Sher? Why can't she see that Shau Feng was right to fight to protect herself against those nerds. She forgets that she did the same when she was young."

Charles went to Shau Feng's room, knocked on the door, and heard a faint voice tell him to enter. He took a long look at her and realized that she could certainly pass for an effeminate boy. Shau Feng's mouth was compressed, with her chin pulled in. Charles winked at her. Puzzled, Shau Feng looked at him.

"Shau Feng, when I bang on the top of this table with my hand, you let out a loud yell."

"Why should I?" she asked.

Charles sighed. "Because I want to prove a point to your aunt—that's why!"

Sher Sher was downstairs with her eyes glued to Shau Feng's door. A loud slam startled her, followed by a scream. Taking two steps at a time up the stairs, she raced, ready for battle. Her hands were compressed into white knuckled fists.

"What did Charles do to the girl?" Bursting into the room, Sher Sher looked for her niece. Shau Feng was standing by the bed. Upon seeing Sher Sher, she giggled. Charles was on the other side of the room, near the window, inspecting his nails. A table near to him was lying on its side.

Shau Feng saw the distressed expression on her aunt's face. She ran and embraced her. In Chinese, the young woman said, "Auntie, I'm sorry." Sher Sher tugged at the girl's short hair. She caressed her niece and glared at her husband over the girl's shoulder.

"Charles, you muttonhead! Some example you set for her. You are incorrigible. This prank of yours almost frightened the life out of me. Let's go downstairs. I need a drink." Shau Feng was released by Sher Sher and left the room. She felt the need of some affection, and so, while going down the stairs, she called Shau De to her. The dog came at a trot and jumped all over her, wagging his tail and licking her. Both went outside to the lawn, where Shau Feng sat with her arms around the Golden Retriever's neck. She recounted the events of the day to him as he sat with his head across her lap in rapt attention.

"Life isn't easy here," said Shau Feng to the dog. Shau De seemed to agree as he snuggled closer to her. "I'm tired of being a child. I wish I were grown up. Does being a lady mean I can never fight for what is right?" At that moment Sher Sher called her to dinner. She suddenly felt hungry. Growing up could wait for the time being.

6

Plainfield College and the China House

Plainfield College was one of the most prestigious private institutions in Ohio. Located ten miles north of Plainfield, it was directly adjacent to Interstate 35. The campus comprised four dormitories: the Texas House, the Caruso House, the Anthony House, and, the most recently built, the China House. Main St. came off the Interstate from the south, went around the campus, and exited a mile north on the same interstate road.

Entrance to the college was by the front gate, and parking lots were on either side of the main street. No outside vehicles were allowed on campus. One had to walk along Main St. to the connecting streets. Once past the parking lots, one walked by the administration building, maintenance shops, college security, the faculty houses, and into the athletic field. Seven years previous, a gymnasium had been built, and Main St. had been extended to encircle the college. At the rear gate were two additional parking lots. These gates were a mile apart. Cherry St., more like a walking path than a street, ran roughly between both main streets, ending at Ash St. The college lecture halls, science lab, cafeteria, and dormitories had streets that crossed both Main and Cherry streets. All streets were tree lined, had lamp-post lighting, benches along the roads, and trash cans every few feet.

Most of the Asian students at Plainfield College resided at the China House. The house was located on Ash St. It was five years old and had been erected with funds provided by the Chinese community of Ohio. The charge for lodging was based on the student's ability to pay. The Lemar Enterprise contributed money to run the house and also subsidized some students through scholarships.

The red-brick house had four levels and a full basement. In the basement were the heating and cooling plants, laundry room, and a large vacant area. The ground level of the house was the living quarters of Mrs. Anna Chou, the house mother. It also had a kitchen, a reception area, library, and a large sitting room. The living quarters of the students were located on the second, third, and fourth floors.

Mrs. Sher Sher Lemar had been instrumental in seeing that Mrs. Chou was hired as house mother, because she had a solid background as an educator and was a retired dean from a New York educational institution. This white-haired attractive woman looked like the Hollywood version of everyone's mother. She loved young people, and, in case of an emergency, she was as solid as a rock in the house. Lastly, the woman was on the same side politically as Mrs. Lemar, and they both belonged to the same educational association.

Knowing Sher Sher Lemar's niece was to attend Plainfield College, in the morning on the day before school started, Diana Wu called upon Shau Feng at the China House. Shau Feng was unpacking in her room, when there was a knock on her door. She answered, "Come in."

Diana Wu entered the room, and Shau Feng saw a young woman of medium height, slender, with long, black, straight hair and a pretty, oval face with a childlike expression.

Diana introduced herself to Shau Feng and said, "Chen Shau Feng, I'm Diana Wu. My mother, Doris Wu, and your Aunt Sher Sher, went to the same academy many years ago in Hong Kong. My grandparents live far away from your grandfather's residence in Hong Kong. Mama asked me to show you around the campus and to assist you in any way, if needed."

"Sit down, please." Shau Feng was removing her clothes from the open suitcases and went about hanging them in the closet.

Observing Shau Feng, Diana felt there was something boyish about her. Shau Feng's appearance seemed to bother her a little, but she dismissed it and said, "Shau Feng, would you like a tour of the campus before it gets dark?"

"Yes, that's a good idea."

While they were walking from Ash St. to Main St. on the campus, Shau Feng said, "Diana, I like your earrings, your rings, your red shoes, and the colorful dress you're wearing."

"My brother-in-law is a jeweler. He gave me the earrings and rings. The dress, I bought in Dayton before coming to college."

"They are very lovely and look well on you."

"Thank you, Shau Feng. Do you know anything about makeup?"

"I'll say I do. My family used to be actors and actresses in the Chinese Opera. I used to watch my grandfather's students apply makeup. Do you want me to teach you how to accent your lips and eyes?"

"That would be fun. Can you cook?"

Shau Feng compressed her lips and made a face. "No, not at all. In Hong Kong, if it wasn't for our housekeeper, Mrs. Kang, I might have died from my own cooking. Anyway, I don't like burned food."

That remark brought a smile to Diana's face, alleviating the nervousness she had felt. "My parents are excellent chefs. Papa is better than Mama. Both my sisters operate frozen-food stores in Columbus, Ohio. Shau Feng, do you like boys?"

"Yes, but, for some unknown reason, they don't seem to like me. I don't think their parents do either. Going to an all-girls school, I didn't get the opportunity to meet a variety of boys. Those I met were elder brothers of classmates."

Feeling a little more comfortable, Diana said, "Boys make me feel very uncomfortable and nervous. They sense my shyness and go out of their way to tease me."

Shau Feng touched her hand. "Diana, boys like to tease shy girls. It's a game they like to play." It struck Shau Feng that Diana had some quality that reminded her of Syang Hwa. They both had the same open, friendly smile and bubbly way of talking. Shau Feng smiled to herself in anticipation of a possible new-found friend.

Diana and Shau Feng walked side by side along Main St. The sky glowed brilliantly golden and reddish in the west. Dormitory lights were on. Faint music could be heard coming from all directions, and students in groups sat on benches along Main St., talking to each other. Further down on Olive St., young men and women were lying on the grass listening to a long-haired youth playing a guitar. Diana passed a remark that the player needed more practice. Shau Feng, suddenly feeling overwhelmed by the newness of everything, remarked, "Do you think I'll get accustomed to it?"

"Sure, pretty soon everything will seem old hat to you. Look—Main St. leads into the athletic field, which is now converted into a football field. My mother told me that your aunt Sher Sher and her husband, Charles, purchased that piece of property behind the athletic field from Mr. Collins and donated it to this college, to build a stadium. The Lemar Construction Company will start building after this football season's over."

Shau Feng said, "Let's go see the place."

Shau Feng stood in the middle of the dirt track that surrounded the football field. She asked Diana if she would like to run, but Diana shook her head no. Shau Feng removed her jacket and tossed it into Diana's arms, and off she ran. With Shau Feng's jacket over her arm, Diana went to sit on a nearby bench. After eight laps, Shau Feng left the track and sat down next to Diana. After a few minutes rest, Shau Feng stood up and did a handstand. Diana applauded energetically. "Shau Feng, I could never do that. You are wonderful."

"Didn't I tell you that all Chens were born Chinese Opera performers? Walking on your hands is not hard. It just takes practice. I'm sure you could do it, if you tried." She put on her jacket, linking her arm with Diana's, and they walked to Main St.

"I'm hungry. Is there any place we can get something to eat?"

"In this area, without a car, there are three places: a cafeteria on the campus, Tabard's Italian food, across from the front gate, and Harry's Deli, a half-mile down the road from the rear gate." While walking, Shau Feng closed her jacket.

"You choose one, Diana, I just want some food to fill my stomach."

Diana didn't like to go to Tabard's because the young men who hung around there always went out of their way to taunt her, and the deli was too far to walk back in the dark. "Shau Feng, let's eat on the campus."

Shau Feng said, "Lead the way."

Diana, at ease with Shau Feng, said, "I seldom made close friends. Before I went to college, Mama kept me at home after school, and so I grew up overly protected and didn't know how to make friends." They both looked at each other for a minute and smiled, each thinking, "Yes, it's going to be a good year."

Shau Feng held the cafeteria door open for Diana to enter. Sounds of swearing drew the young women's attention to a table not far away from the cafeteria entrance. They saw two American youths taunting a seated Chinese young man who wore thick glasses. In a very loud voice, one of the bullies insulted their prey. Brian was six feet, husky, with a thick head of hair, and a big, thick nose. He grabbed the sandwich from the tray in front of the Chinese student and threw it in the trash can. His action was met with a stone face from the Chinese youth. Feeling encouraged, Brian pushed a pile of books off the student's table to the floor. Diana whispered in Shau Feng's ear, "Those two animals, Brian and David, always pick on Chinese. They beat up Tom Lee last semester, giving him a black eye and a bloody nose for no reason at all. Tom is such a gentle soul. He wouldn't hurt a fly. Now they are after Bruce Tong."

Feeling a need to help the victim, Shau Feng moved swiftly with power and strength. She hated bullies and headed for the youth, yelling in excellent English, "You two, pick up those books!"

The young men turned to face Shau Feng, who was a few feet away from them. They saw a five-foot-six-inch, 115-lb. Chinese person wearing a red jacket and a Greek fisherman's cap. The boys sneered at their smaller challenger. Brian's face took on a sadistic grin. "Lookie here.... Another monkey." David scoffed, "Hey, shit-for-brains, my prick is bigger than you. Are you standing in a hole?" David stood five foot eight, soft of body, with acne all over his face.

Brian picked up the cue. "Say, doesn't it hurt to stand on your hind legs and act like a man?" They laughed, staring at Shau Feng.

She sarcastically replied, "I didn't know dummies could talk. Pick up those books now!"

Brian, contemptuous of his smaller opponent, aggressively moved forward, reaching out with his right hand to grab Shau Feng's jacket. He growled, "Come to Papa, little man, I'm going to spread your nose all over your face!"

Shau Feng crossed her arms under Brian's outstretched arm to raise them. She kicked him in the belly. The shock caused Brian to shriek and double over. Shau Feng aimed a punch, which landed on his nose. Backwards Brian fell, with a thud. As he lay lying on the floor, a steady stream of profanity flowed from his mouth as Shau Feng looked at his face. Shau Feng let go with a second punch, hitting his eye. "This one is for Tom Lee." David, standing next to Bruce's table, froze in his tracks. His mouth was dry, and his knees began to shake. He saw that Brian was bleeding from his nose, and his eye was tearing. Shau Feng made a threatening move toward David.

"Pick up the books and pile them neatly on the table, or it's your turn, Cowboy!" Down he went on one knee, collecting the books. Shau Feng slapped David on the back of the head and said, "I recall seeing a sandwich on the tray. Buy another one right now, and put it on the table!" When she heard Brian still cursing, Shau Feng shouted, "Bloody yank bastard, if you don't stop bad-mouthing people, I'll wash your mouth out with soapy dishwater! I see your mama and papa neglected to teach you manners, but I can." Brian touched his aching nose with his hand. It came away bloody. Placing her right fist inside her left palm, she said, "My name is Chen Shau Feng. I reside at the China House. Leave the Chinese students in peace, or you can expect more of what you got today! Now get out of my sight." David didn't look at Brian as he helped him to his feet and out the door.

"Where the fuck did this one come from?"

The small crowd cheered the brave Chinese youth, but Shau Feng paid them no mind. The female cashier hurried to Shau Feng, to warn her about Brian and his friends, who would come to seek revenge. Shau Feng told the woman not to worry. When Diana heard what the cashier had said, she pleaded with Shau Feng in Chinese to return to the China House with her. Shau Feng ignored Diana's warnings and asked her to calm herself. To divert Diana's mind, Shau Feng asked to be introduced to the young Chinese man. Diana introduced Shau Feng to Bruce Tong, who recognized the skill of a veteran fighter in Shau Feng. When Diana asked Shau Feng again to return to the China House, she replied, "Diana, go back to the China House yourself if you are afraid. I won't hold it against you. I have never run away from any trouble. I'm not going to start now."

Bruce mumbled apologetically, "I will stand by you, Shau Feng, but I don't know how to fight." The young man hung his head in shame.

Shau Feng touched his arm. "Honest, Mr. Tong, I don't need anyone's help."

Diana looked pale and shaken. She said, "Shau Feng, I'll not leave this place without you."

Paul Armstrong was Plainfield's newly acquired quarterback from Tennessee State College and a part-time worker in the campus cafeteria. He was just a little over six feet, husky, blond, with classical facial features. The young man had witnessed the entire episode from behind the counter, where he worked. Paul admired the spunk and courage of the Chinese youth. He knew that the troublemakers, Brian and David, were furious at being beaten and would lose no time in seeking retaliation. Always on the side of the underdog, Paul made a mental note to be on Shau Feng's side, in case he was needed. Paul went to his locker, changed his clothes, and took a seat at a table behind the Chinese trio. Another football player for the Plainfield Lions, Jim Hawkins, who also worked behind the counter, joined Paul at the table, not taking the time to change his clothes.

In the cafeteria, the students who had witnessed the fight whispered among themselves across their tables, but kept an eye on the swinging front doors. Bruce reasoned that, if those guys returned with their friends, they too would be sorry. Bruce believed that most Americans were beasts. The beating Brian had gotten couldn't have happened to a more deserving person.

Less than fifteen minutes later, there were five young men outside the campus cafeteria. Brian and David had talked their friends into going to the cafeteria to beat up his attackers. Bill, tall and husky, with a face full of freckles, pushed the swinging doors open and bellowed through his buck teeth, "Where are the guys who hit Brian? Crawl out of your hiding place!"

Shau Feng rose and replied, "Windbag, save your bad breath. I'm the one." His eyes opened wide to see a short, thin Chinese in an oversized red jacket. Shau Feng continued, "Let's go outside, big boy."

Outside, Shau Feng stood several feet away from the five youths, eyeing the group and saying, "What a scroungy lot you are! Did your friends find you in the garbage can? I'll take you on one at a time or all at once. It's your choice. How do you want your lumps?"

Paul Armstrong shoved his way through the crowd to stand beside Shau Feng and said, "Gentlemen, I don't like the odds. Let's even them."

Shau Feng stepped closer to Paul and whispered from the side of her mouth, "Shove off, Yank. I don't need your help. Do you think this is a cowboy-and-Indian movie?"

Paul replied, "I don't remember offering you any help. This is a free country. Anyway, cowboy heroes wear white hats—not that stupid one you have on your head." The five young men looked at each other. They didn't mind fighting against one person, but two was a different story. Mike charged forward. Paul, using a football block, knocked him down and followed it up with an elbow smash to the face. Mike, of medium height, sported a crew cut and looked like a bulldog with a small nose. A second punch to the jaw by Paul took the fight out of him. Mike lay on the ground, dazed.

William came running to help Mike and leaped on Paul's back. They fell to the ground, rolling and grabbing at each other. William was inches taller than Paul, heavyset and with thin legs. As she watched the action, Shau Feng was puzzled. It crossed her mind that neither of them knew how to fight. Shau Feng advanced toward Bill, who assumed a karate-kicking stance. Rubbing her nose with a finger, Shau Feng circled around him, while keeping an eye on the other youths. It caused Bill to alter his position constantly. Meanwhile, on the move, Shau Feng was sinking low. Bill settled in a double weight stance, waved his long arm, and flexed his finger in Shau Feng's face. She came in rapidly, kicking sharply at his fingers. The impact stung him and resulted in a quick withdrawal of the hand. Shau Feng continued her attack with a series of kicks, which landed on Bill's chest and lower ribcage. The foot circled to strike his shin and rose to hit his chest again. Bill went backward, landing on the ground. Shau Feng advanced and rapped him in the left eye.

"Motherfucker! Jesus Christ!" he yelled, covering his face with his hands as the pain shot through his body. Shau Feng glanced over her shoulder to see how Paul had fared. They were evenly matched in strength. Neither had the advantage over the other, as they rolled about on the ground. Shau Feng merely shook her head.

Jeff, a tall, beefy youth with a clear complexion, charged Shau Feng like a wild dog. He intended to use his greater weight to knock Shau Feng off her feet. She saw Jeff coming fast with his head low and arms stretched out. At the last second, before Jeff could have made contact with her, Shau Feng sidestepped him. She chopped hard with the side of her hand against the back of his neck. The blow drove Jeff into the ground. He attempted to rise, not knowing Shau Feng was coming at him, cartwheeling. As Jeff staggered to his feet, Shau Feng double-punched both his eyes and followed with a blow to the jaw. Glassy-eyed, Jeff stared ahead as he sank to the ground.

Meanwhile, Paul and William had each other by the ears. William spat in Paul's face. It resulted in Paul's twisting his nose. That picture amused Shau Feng. She wondered if they would bite off each other's nose or ear. Shau Feng directed her attention to Eric, who had assumed a boxer's stance. Eric bounced around on his toes. The tall and slender young man threw jabs at Shau Feng's face. His long arms gave him a greater reach over Shau Feng. She taunted Eric, "You can't hit me if you are that far away. Maybe if you move fast enough around me, I'll get dizzy and faint. Did your mother teach you how to box, little boy?" Eric's face turned brick red because of the insult. He came swinging. Shau Feng waited until Eric was within the range of her foot. Off the ground, it came, striking the young man's shin. The pain shot through his body, and Eric grabbed for the leg. Shau Feng socked him in the jaw with a series of punches. Her slap on his face made a loud noise. Eric was still standing. Shau Feng dropped him with a solid kick to the chest.

She surveyed the field of battle. Mike, Paul's challenger, was getting to his feet. A series of forward flips brought her to the youth. She drop-kicked Mike, who flew fifteen feet back before hitting the ground.

"Too strong," she told herself. "You don't want to break the creep's bones. All you want is to let them look terrible for the next few days." This time, Mike made no effort to rise. The kick had hurt him. Shau Feng rotated her cap so the visor was at the back of her head. She rubbed the side of her nose with two fingers, unconsciously portraying a boy.

Using peripheral vision, she saw Paul was still grappling with his opponent. Boldly she strutted over to them. Shau Feng grabbed William's thumb, twisting it. Paul, feeling himself freed, punched his opponent hard in the jaw. He sank to the ground. Shau Feng released the thumb. Strutting around, she loudly announced to the crowd, "Tell all your friends not to assault or pick on any Chinese on this campus, or they will receive the same treatment those characters got," pointing to Jeff, lying on the ground looking at her. "You have a choice: Either get up and continue to fight, or get the bloody hell out of my sight." Shau Feng had given the young men a way out. Before they retreated, she declared, "My name is Chen Shau Feng. I reside at the China House. I'm not hard to find." From the crowd came a cheer for the courageous Chinese. Others in the crowd helped the defeated youths from the Texas House stand up.

The spectators had never seen any young person who could fight with so much skill, and they naturally mistook Shau Feng for a boy by her appearance and dress. One young woman asked her friend, "Isn't that little Chinese boy like the hero in a chop-them-up film?" Soon the spectators were asking each other the Chinese youth's name. One replied, "Chen something."

Breathing hard from the exertion, Paul was on his feet, examining his pants. Exhibiting no effects from the fight, Shau Feng went over to Paul. His face was bruised, his lower lip cut, and he was still pumped up from the action. Slowly they took each other's measure. Paul said, "I was doing okay by myself. Why couldn't you mind your own business?" Shau Feng politely replied, "Chen Shau Feng at your service. I'm grateful for your help, and I'm in your debt. Thank you. If you ever need my help, I can be found at the China House."

Paul wasn't expecting this kindness from the Chinese youth. He couldn't remain angry with him. "You're welcome, boy."

Shau Feng shot back, her eyes widening, "I'm not a boy!"

Paul defensively raised his hands. "I stand corrected. Look—I got the first part of your name—Chen. What is the last part?" Bruce came forward and answered for Shau Feng.

"Chen is the surname. Shau Feng is the given name. It means 'Little Phoenix.'" Paul grinned broadly, extending his right hand.

"You're not little in my dictionary! Put it here, Phoenix."

Bruce led Diana and Shau Feng away from the cafeteria to the China House. He was attracted to Shau Feng; therefore he wanted to get her away from Paul. Left behind, standing still, Paul watched the three Chinese youths walking away.

"How did I do, Diana?" Her face registered admiration.

"Oh, you are a genuine heroine. You had them beat, hands down, but you scared me to death. Why did you bruise their faces?"

"Diana, I made them an example. Others, seeing them, will think twice before picking a fight with a Chinese. I'm not in favor of fighting as a way of life, but in this imperfect world, the strong sometimes eat up the weak. There are some people who ask for a finger, and then take your entire arm." Shau Feng smiled as she quoted her grandfather perfectly.

Bruce stammered, "Miss Chen, you are extraordinary. Thank you for rescuing me. I shall always be in your debt. May I be further in debt, by having you teach me how to defend myself?"

As they were walking, she was thinking over Bruce's request.

Before reaching the China House, Shau Feng made up her mind. She said, "Mr. Tong, I'll teach you or any Chinese who are willing to learn Kung Fu, but first, we must find a place to practice."

"Miss Chen, there is such a place in the basement in the China House."

Climbing the stairs leading to the cafeteria, Paul looked over his shoulder, continuing to peer at Phoenix and her friends until they were out of his sight. He thought, "All my life, I have found it difficult to communicate with strangers. Now that I had an opportunity to speak, I was at a loss for words and forgot to tell Phoenix my name."

Entering the cafeteria, Paul sat at a table to catch his breath and collect his thoughts. Jim Hawkins walked along the food line and set two dinners on his tray with two drinks. He too had watched the fight. The youth set the tray on the table and sat across from Paul. Paul said to him, "What is so funny these days?"

"Hey, Do-gooder, I thought you told me the other day you only minded your own business. You red-neck Kentucky hillbilly—what do you call that stunt outside?"

Paul looked at a smiling Jim. He reacted by breaking into a grin. Jim said, "Buy you supper, Old Dog." Paul took no offense at the words of the big young black man. Jim was good-natured and treated him well. He had the gift of gab that Paul admired. He took the meat plate and flatware off Jim's tray.

"I couldn't let the little shrimp fight those big guys alone," Jim laughed scornfully.

"Backwoods jackass—you assumed too much. That Kung Fu-er never needed your help. In fact, you were in the way. Phoenix was taught by a real martial-arts master, not the ones you saw around here or in the movies. He bruised them for effect, but took special care not to injure those jerks." Paul's face showed dejection. He couldn't eat and just played with his food.

Jim saw that Paul was downcast and started to console him. "These are hard times for heroes, Old Buddy. Come—dry your tears. Lick your wounds, count your scars, and eat. Your good intention still deserves bragging rights."

On the way to the China House, Shau Feng inquired, "Who is the blond guy, and why did he shorten my name? He also thought I was a boy—now isn't that a laugh?"

Bruce replied, "His name is Paul Armstrong. He is the college's new football quarterback, who came from Tennessee State College. Americans have the habit of shortening a person's name or giving him nicknames. Like most Americans I know, he has no manners. Why, he didn't even introduce himself after you rescued his hide. Americans aren't like Chinese. They are very outgoing and rude. And, my dear, you sure do look like a boy."

Joining the conversation, Diana said, "Our new coach, Chet Harris, is building a completely new football team for the college. He is also the brother-in-law of the president of the college, Dr. Oriello. Chet is known as "Pop" by the people who play for him. He was a Hall-of-Fame football college coach, who came out of retirement. Paul Armstrong is the Lions' new quarterback." Shau Feng's mind was elsewhere. She wasn't paying attention to Diana. She couldn't imagine what had prompted Paul to help her. One thing was certain; this Paul didn't know how to fight. Grandfather had been right. Americans were crazy people. She said, "Diana, I'm starving. Is there any Chinese food in this place?"

Bruce said, in Chinese, "I have some Chinese food in my room. Allow me to feed you."

"Okay, but I will not go to your room without Diana."

"No problem, I have more than enough food for three. I can even cook a little."

In the living room, stretched out on an oversize chair, Charles scanned the sports section of the local daily newspaper. Sher Sher, in a low voice, was talking in Chinese to someone on the phone. While she was talking, every so often, she glanced at Charles. After hanging up, Sher Sher called Charles. He raised his head from the newspaper. Sher Sher, sitting very straight in her chair, informed him that Shau Feng had had a fight at the campus. He asked, "Was she hurt?" Sher Sher shook her head.

"What was the fight about?" She told him the reason for the battle and repeated with mixed feelings that, as a young girl, she would have acted as aggressively as Shau Feng. But she also had a responsibility: to help Shau Feng develop her feminine characteristics. She sought Charles's help.

"What should we do?"

He calmly said, "Those dumb oxen got a good lesson. Some people just can't stop annoying others, unless they get a smack in the face." From the look on Sher Sher's face, he knew that wasn't the response she wanted to hear. He altered his approach. "Do you want me to take a ride to Plainfield College and introduce myself to the young men at the Texas House? I'll just shake hands. No violence, I promise—my word of honor."

Charles closed his big hands. The muscles bulged on his forearm.

Sher Sher wasn't concerned with the beaten youths. If she were, she would have gone herself to the college, to break some necks if her niece were harmed. She punched her left palm with her right fist. "Wow—Shau Feng sure has nerve—five against two!" Charles's eyebrows went up. Sher Sher smiled at him. "Although she really ought to control herself. Charles, I want you to help me teach her how to act more like a lady!"

Charles rose, towering over her, asserted, "Does being a lady mean she can't defend herself when attacked? Does it mean a lady can't fight for justice? Have you taken into consideration the reason for the fight? The youth of the world can't stand injustice. Your father knew what he was doing when he trained that young woman.

How much martial-arts training did your father give you?"

Sher Sher gave Charles a shove, which didn't budge him. She had a stern look on her face. "You miss the entire point, as usual. Could you listen for once, and do as I ask?"

He replied, "Woman, do you realize how you are asserting yourself now?" Her eyes twinkled as she smothered a giggle.

"Shau Feng has courage, a sense of right and wrong, and a kind heart. How many people would stand up to a bully to protect someone else? Don't confine her to a cage. Give Shau Feng space to grow. You will see—she will develop into a fine human being." Sher Sher wrapped her arms around his neck, as he bent to kiss her. Charles continued, "Love, I realize the difficulty of being a bystander. You don't want to see those you love get hurt. Shau Feng must learn her own lessons. That is the way of life." Tenderly she touched his face. They found their way to the bedroom and made love for a long time that night.

In the China House, after returning to her room, Shau Feng prepared a bath. She stood in front of the mirror, turning right to left examining her body, saying, "Do I really look that much like a boy? That blond guy is very stupid. Couldn't he see that I don't have an Adam's Apple?" She put on a nightgown. As an afterthought, Shau Feng called her grandfather in Hong Kong. She described the fight to him and what had led up to it. When her grandfather had been reassured that she wasn't hurt, he felt relieved. She said, "I couldn't stand idly by and watch a defenseless person be beaten, especially my own countryman."

Lee replied, "The world we live in isn't a storybook. Everyone has his own ambitions and ego. This makes some act aggressive and others defensive when they feel threatened. Being a protector is wonderful, but it isn't your life's goal. Study hard to make the Chen name a beacon for others." A tear came to his eyes. "I'm very proud of you."

"Grandfather, you were wrong about Uncle Charles. He likes me very much, and, by the way, the dog, Shau De, likes me too.

Before school started, Shau De and I use to run every day together. Why was it that we never had a dog?"

He replied, "Because I'm allergic to dogs. Good night, Shau Feng."

7

The Plainfield Lions

It was 5:00 A.M. Chet Harris, the football coach of Plainfield College, dressed and walked down the stairs very quietly so as not to disturb his wife, Lois. He always had a problem sleeping when the football season started, and the new season was just six weeks away. The college football team had been losing games for the past three years, and it was generally known around the college that President Gabriella Oriello was fired up to produce a winning team this year.

Wearing a Plainfield Lions jacket and cap, Chet walked out of his house and headed for the football field. Once there, he sat on a bench to light his pipe and ponder his problems. He watched a morning runner and felt nostalgic about the physical prowess of his youth having diminished. He wished some magic could make his body young again. His focus centered on the lone runner, who seemed to be moving at a fast pace, making excellent time. That young runner was Shau Feng.

Her restlessness was due to being homesick for Hong Kong and the cultural shock of being in such a different country. Running was an emotional outlet that invigorated her. Sensing an accumulated supply of energy flowing into her body, she abruptly increased her speed, at the same time releasing a yell. At that moment, she caught all of Chet's attention.

"Hmm," he commented to himself. "Very good." The runner's rate of acceleration brought Chet to his feet. It electrified him. He said, "Jesus, it's a coach's dream come true." He headed to the track.

There he waved his arms wildly. When the runner came near a streetlight, Chet said to himself, "Isn't that Phoenix Chen? Sure it is.... Young Jack Ranger pointed him out to me last week, down Main St., and said that Phoenix had whipped the ass of seven nerds with help from Paul. A runner with that kind of speed could be the key to our championship."

Shau Feng saw the man waving his arms. She recognized the football coach, because tall Terry had pointed him out to her during lunch last Friday. When she was ten yards from the man, she slowed down to a trot.

"Good morning. I'm Chet Harris."

"Good morning to you, sir. I know who you are." Shau Feng was breathing deeply.

Chet couldn't contain his eagerness. His voice trembled as he spoke. "Phoenix, how would you like to play football? You are the fastest runner I have ever seen in my forty-odd years." A surprised look came to her face. Words stumbled out of her mouth, "Sir, I only like to run."

"Nonsense, boy ... "

Shau Feng pulled in her chin. "I'm not a boy, sir!"

"Don't get your dander up! It's only a figure of speech. Phoenix, how would you like to be the first Chinese to play football on a college team? The team needs a person with your speed. It could mean the key between winning and losing. A gift like yours comes once in a lifetime to an old coot like me. The newspapers call me a dinosaur and an over-the-hill coach. I should have stayed retired, but there is still a flame inside me that burns to work with young people." Chet removed his pipe from his mouth. When he saw tears in Phoenix's eyes, he knew the youth had been touched by his words. An overwhelming feeling of desperation caused Chet to press on. He wanted a yes for an answer. Shau Feng didn't take in everything Chet said, but, deep down, she knew that the old man needed her help in some way. The pipe smoke triggered a memory of her cigar-smoking grandfather, and she remembered the final words they had spoken to each other: "Grandfather, I'll always remember what you taught me. I will try to bring honor to the Chen name and always come to the aid of others who need help."

Not knowing what to say, she blinked her eyes while Chet was standing there with his pipe in his hand, and she requested time to think over the offer. Finally she said, "If I agree to play football, I'll come to Monday's team practice." Shau Feng reflected as she trotted away from the track. "Should I tell Mr. Harris that I'm a girl? Perhaps I ought to call Grandfather for a consultation before I say yes." She was tingling with excitement.

Chet called out, "See you on Monday, Phoenix." His gut feeling was that the boy would be there Monday. He could smell the championship. "That youth will make football history," he said. Chet relit his pipe, heading for home in a happier frame of mind than when he had left home in the morning. Chet knew very well that a failure could not only end his dream, but Gabriella's and the college's reputation. Chet looked up at the sky. He saw the sun was on the rise. "An omen," he said. "My gloomy days of retirement will be over. It isn't all it's cracked up to be. It's good to be in the active life again."

It was Sunday morning. After the Kung Fu class, Shau Feng went to Diana's room, which she shared with two other young women. Most of the young women at the China House would congregate there on the weekends. While chatting and eating, Shau Feng related that Chet Harris had asked her to play football for the Lions. She stated, "He saw me running and is under the impression I'm a boy. Girls can't play football on a Boys' team."

The strikingly attractive Sara Sing, tall, with short, curly hair and a model's body, said, "That isn't exactly true, Shau Feng. Nowhere in the football rule book does it state that you have to be male to play football. The offer from Mr. Harris gives you a great opportunity to bring the Chinese students at this college much honor. He wants a victory very much. It would put our college on a par with the big colleges. He just might let you play as a female if we won. Just think of all the great worldwide publicity—for him as well as for us. Actually, it would be very difficult to hide yourself from him. Why not let him make the decision? Years before, in this college, we had a professor, Dr. Wang Man Ching, who won a Nobel Prize in Literature for writing the book *I-Ching and the Universe*. After she won the prize, it was discovered by a reporter who came for an interview that Dr. Wang was a woman. Dr. Wang brought honor to the Chinese. I think Chet's offer is great. The first Chinese in the record book to play college football is a female. Shau Feng, just disguise yourself, and act like a young man. Who is going to tell the Americans anything different? You can count on us to keep the secret."

Mimi said, "The Chinese boys would be only too glad to rub it in the Americans' noses once the truth comes out. In Chinese history, there were times when women, disguised as a man, rose to save their nation."

Jo-An, who looked like a little girl, declared, "The macho males merely think a woman's place is in the home or between the sheets. Times have changed. The world is waking up to a new day."

Shau Feng was pleased with the response she received and said, "Friends, if I masquerade as a boy, it can't be done without cooperation. I'm willing to play football for the glory of my fellow countrymen and my family, but you all must support me." She looked in each girl's face. "Can I count on you?" They leaped to their feet, shouting their support and chanting, "We'll guard you with our lives." Amid peals of laughter, the helpful hints came almost one on top of the other, "Keep your eyes steady. Don't look about for approval. Look with a sense of self-containment—comfortable in your own space."

"Lower your voice an octave."

"No smiling—no giggling. Laugh out loud."

"Cut your hair short, and slick your hair with gel."

"Bind your breasts with an ace bandage."

"When you talk, speak in short statements. Make demands. Give orders."

"When you take a drink from a glass, use your whole hand to hold it, as if it weighed a ton."

"Spread your feet apart when sitting down."

Mimi asserted, "Shau Feng, my brother is a doctor. He will fill out any paper the college gives you." They gathered around Shau Feng, saying, "Yes . . . yes . . . yes."

Sunday night, Shau Feng phoned her grandfather. She told him about the offer that the football coach, Mr. Chet Harris, had made to her. Her grandfather said, "I think you should accept Mr. Harris' invitation. You will be honoring your ancestors, your school, and yourself as a woman. But Mr. Harris must know about it. We should not deceive him. I will speak to him personally on the phone. Together, he and I will map out a strategy for you. I will also talk to your uncle and aunt. They will be your support behind the scenes. You can do it by using your acting ability to create an illusion in which people see a male image. Ma Lan, who replaced her father, fought on the battlefield and was never detected to be a female. Since your American uncle taught you the game, follow his advice and win." Shau Feng was very happy that her grandfather backed her decision. The old master increased her monthly pocket money, so she could buy anything she wanted. Shau Feng missed him dearly.

Before going to bed, Shau Feng prayed, clapping her hands together to attract the gods' attention. She asked the goddess of love and mercy for help in the task that lay ahead. Shau Feng said, "Kuan Yin, guide me, guard me, and protect me. Help me with what I have to do as I meet with Mr. Harris on Monday."

After years of associating with Chet, Joe and Wilton were familiar with all his quirks and habits. On Monday, Chet had the lifeguard stand moved from one side of the field to the other. This puzzled Joe and Wilton. Chet was a creature of habit. He always had his lifeguard stand facing away from a path to the football field, for luck. They surmised that he expected someone unusual to come. Joe Brown put the young football players through a warm-up drill. Wilton Claymore assembled his squads and took them through a running game. Mr. Brown instructed the quarterbacks and receivers in ball-handling and field position. Joe was impressed with the way Paul threw the ball. It was quick and accurate. Bobby Gold, the second-string quarterback, was good, but needed confidence and experience. He tensed under pressure and often neglected to take time to look over the field before throwing. Every so often, Joe and Wilton glanced at Chet, who was on the lifeguard stand. His attention was off in the distance. Again, he returned his glance from the football field to Main St. A grin exploded across his face. Down he came from the stand to the ground. He whistled an old tune. Chet called out. "Mr. Gold, come over here, and bring a football with you." Chet's rapid descent caught his assistant coaches' eyes. They followed his gaze to Main St. Chet had been looking at two Chinese students; One was a girl, by the way she was dressed and walked. The other was a boy whom they didn't recognize. Shau Feng was wearing a dark-blue oversized sweatsuit and white running shoes. The Greek fisherman's cap went on her head when she got close to the field. Diana took a seat on the benches. Shau Feng trotted onto the field. Brown came over to Claymore and asked, "Joe, do you recognize that kid?"

"No, all Chinese look alike to me."

Shau Feng walked toward Chet Harris with her cap pulled down over her ears. Bob was standing near Chet. Shau Feng said to Chet, "Sorry I'm late, sir. I am here to play football if you still want me?"

Chet motioned to her to step aside so that they could speak quietly away from the others. When they were out of hearing distance, he spoke. "Phoenix, I have given the matter a great deal of thought. After I conversed with your venerable grandfather and discussed it further with my wife, I feel privileged to be in your confidence and agree to your joining the football team. You will attend classes and be on the football team as a male. I assume your fellow Chinese living in the China House will guard your secret carefully."

Shau Feng grinned, "They'll go to their death before betraying me."

The football coach continued, "While training and playing football, you will be under the care of my wife and me. The team will be told that you are making a recovery from a rare, but not life-threatening nor infectious disease, and must lie down quietly after taking your medicine. Your aunt and uncle can take care of your medical records." He touched her gently on the arm and said, "Your grandfather informed me that 'Lying isn't bad if it is for a good cause in the larger scheme of things.' How about it, Phoenix? Do we have a deal?"

Choking back her tears, Shau Feng slowly nodded her head, quietly thanking her grandfather and Kwan Yin. They walked back to the group and were immediately surrounded by the young men.

"Welcome to the Lions, Phoenix. This is Bobby Gold." They nodded at each other. "Kid, can you catch a football?" They all started talking at the same time.

"I'll give it a try." Bobby and Phoenix lobbed the ball back and forth a few times. Then they began to increase the distance between them. Soon Bobby went from simple tosses to bullet passes. Chet saw the Chinese kid pull them all down. She didn't drop one within her reach. Gold's enthusiasm soared as he watched Phoenix leap high into the air to catch the ball, one-handed. He tossed the ball way over his head. The kid reached the ball and caught it. Chet guessed where this young Chinese learned to catch a football like a pro and whistled off key, with a grin spreading across his face.

The center snapped the ball to Paul, who went back a few steps and threw it to Robin, running down the sidelines. Paul turned his head to look over his shoulder. He saw Phoenix was catching a football. Paul's eyes scanned the benches around the field, and there he located Diana. It was unbelievable, the stories that the guys told about Diana's being extremely boy-shy. If they were true, why was she hanging around Phoenix all the time? She wasn't boy-shy at all with Phoenix.

Robin, Paul's intended receiver, momentarily glanced at Phoenix, who was running. With his concentration broken, the ball bounced out of his outstretched hands. Claymore yelled, "Robin, keep your mind focused!"

As a child, Shau Feng had been taught by her grandfather to catch any object thrown at her. In the past three months, her Uncle Charles had further sharpened that skill, by having her practice catching a football. When Chet noticed that the players had stopped to watch Phoenix, he shouted, "Phoenix, Bobby, that's enough. Come here please." Bobby was highly charged from Phoenix's fine performance. He whooped, howled, bellowed, then strutted about, letting loose with a rebel yell.

He said, "Phoenix, you are sensational!" Shau Feng didn't understand his thick, Southern-accented words. Suddenly, he charged at her, throwing a high five at the last minute. Training caused Shau Feng to act just as Bobby's hand came to her. Bobby went sailing over Shau Feng's shoulder and landed on his back. He attempted to rise, only to have a football hit him on the chest. Paul had thrown the ball to keep Bobby down, in case he went for Phoenix. Paul came running to stand between Phoenix and Bobby. Bobby, holding out his hands, asked, "What did I do?"

Paul said, "Phoenix, what seems to be the problem?"

Shau Feng declared, "Did you hear the strange sounds coming out of Mr. Gold's mouth and see the odd way he acted? Has he gone mad?"

Paul's face brightened into a smile. He replied, "Those sounds you heard came from loose marbles, rolling around in his Southern head. Believe it or not, Phoenix, the strange language is English." The guys laughed. Bobby's face flushed, turning scarlet. Harry bent to retrieve Bobby's glasses from the ground and handed them to him.

Shau Feng said, "Please tell me what he said in plain English."

Bobby's face registered irritation, caused by being the brunt of the guy's coarse humor. When Shau Feng realized her mistake, she stepped forward to face Bobby and said, "Mr. Gold, please accept my apology for being rude. I'm fresh off the plane from Hong Kong and don't fully grasp your language or your American ways. Please overlook my ignorance, and help me in the future to better understand you."

Bobby looked at the Chinese youth in wonderment. He had heard the punter talk about Phoenix's fighting ability and didn't quite know what to make of this young Chinese man. In his nineteen years, nobody had ever been this gracious to him, or apologized to him in public. The young Southerner wasn't going to be outdone by this Chinese kid. He said, "Phoenix, I'm equally to be blamed. Here's my hand. Give me a high five." They smiled at each other, touching hands lightly.

Chet said, "It's good that you settled this misunderstanding like gentlemen." Turning to Shau Feng, Chet asked, "Lad, where did you learn to catch a football?"

"From my uncle, Charles Lemar...." Joe and Wilton wondered what else Charles Lemar, who'd been known as "the Dutchman," taught this Chinese kid. They remembered seeing the big guy in action years ago. At that time, he had been playing pro ball for the New York Rams. The big guy had been unstoppable and a brilliant play reader. When Chet asked Brown to select the five fastest runners on the team, Phoenix was one of them.

On the track, Robin was next to Phoenix. He was slightly under six feet and wiry, with thick, dark-brown hair and long legs. He was the fastest sprinter on the squad. Robin enjoyed telling jokes and playing pranks. He said to Phoenix in a low voice, "Hey, Little Shrimp, take a good look at my rear. When this race is in progress, that will be in your face."

Shau Feng was exhilarated by the challenge. She called to Brown, "Please wait a minute." Off she trotted to where Diana was sitting. Diana said to her friend, "Shau Feng, you are remarkable."

"Thanks. Would you give me the white pompom from your hat? I want to attach it to the rear of my sweatsuit." Diana did as Shau Feng asked. "See you soon," said Shau Feng, and she was off.

Watching her friend catching a football, Diana was awed. Never in her life had she seen anyone like Shau Feng. In the short time that she had known her, Shau Feng had already stepped in to protect her against the annoying young men. So, when Diana had seen Shau Feng drop Bobby Gold, she didn't blink an eye, because she had grown accustomed to her friend's ways.

Shau Feng returned to Robin, taunting him, "Round Eyes, small ears and big nose, see this bunny tail? That will guide this pack of pups through my dust." Robin smiled, declaring, "Jellybean, I'll have that cottontail between my teeth within twenty yards." Brown lined up the boys and blew his whistle. Breaking away from the pack, increasing the lead with every step, Shau Feng was flying over the ground. When the race was over, she turned to thumb her nose at Robin. He gave her the victory sign and a little bow.

Paul worked his way through the players to stand next to Phoenix. He intentionally bumped Shau Feng with his hip. Shau Feng turned, giving him a look, and said, "I hope you can play football better than you fight!"

"Little Squirt, you'll need a flag attached to your helmet for me to find you." He playfully placed his foot on her sneaker. Shau Feng shoved him away. After introducing Shau Feng as Phoenix, Chet dismissed the team for the evening, and Claymore walked over to Shau Feng.

"Phoenix, tomorrow I'll give you our playbook and equipment."

"Sir, I would like to have number 44."

"Okay, can do...." Off Shau Feng ran to Diana.

Bronco and Harry walked together with Robin to the Caruso House. Bronco was six-foot-one, husky, with shoulder-length, light-brown hair, and a square face dominated by a broad handlebar mustache. Harry, his cousin, was slightly shorter, ugly, with a face that looked chiseled from stone. He was built like a teddy bear, with thick, muscular arms and short hair. Harry commented, "Speedster, what do you think of the new kid on the block?" Robin placed an arm around Harry's neck.

"This team has two birds, one with wings on its back, and the other one with wings on its feet. That spunky Chinese kid is the edge we talked about last week. The opposition will need their entire backfield to cover him or try to attack-dog him. Our job is to insure they don't succeed. I played this college circuit for a year. Believe me, there is nobody out there faster than Phoenix. Phoenix has world-class speed." With a pleased look, Robin added, "Man alive, are we going to eat up the opposition and kick a lot of butt this season."

Casi Gomez and Jim Hawkins were a few yards behind the rest of the team, heading for the dorm. Casi was six feet, with a broad chest and thick, jet-black hair and dark eyes. The Latin youth considered himself to be God's gift to women. He ogled every woman who passed him.

Paul was a shy person. He had been raised on a farm. He and his brothers had helped their parents after school, and there had been time for them to play with the neighbors' children. In the past, it had always been difficult for him to warm up to strangers. The guys whom he played football with were different; they shared a common bond. Paul felt that, if he didn't play football, they wouldn't act friendly toward him. He compared himself to Casi and Jim, believing that he wasn't as quick in learning as they were. Feeling inferior, he put extra effort into his studies. The driving force behind this was the spirit of his late mother. On her deathbed, she had made him promise to pursue a college education.

Back on the campus, Joe couldn't contain his excitement.

"I timed the Chinese kid while he ran. He tied the world record today. Do you think there is something wrong with my stopwatch?" Chet placed an arm on Joe's back. He whistled a tune.

"Yes, I know how fast Phoenix can run. Besides, I'll bet his uncle, Charles Lemar, taught him more than just how to catch a football."

Wilton remarked, "In that case, I'll buy both of you a meatball and spaghetti dinner if we have a losing season."

Joe laughed, "We have with us the last of the big-time spenders. Just between us, Joe, how deep do your pockets go?"

Chet was grinning. He said, "Don't make fun of yesterday's big lottery winner."

It had become Diana's habit to speak Chinese whenever she was alone with Shau Feng. Shau Feng was elated that she had outrun Robin. She wasn't aware that Robin had been the second-fastest runner during last year's football season. Shau Feng didn't even know Robin was a high-school track star. To Shau Feng, it was just good clean fun.

On the way to the China House, Diana said, "I think that blond guy likes you."

"Paul seems nice, but too bad he isn't Chinese. Anyway, that blond dope thinks I'm a boy." Diana gave Shau Feng a look, closing an eye.

Shau Feng saw it and giggled. "You know something? I like him too."

During the practice session, Paul began showing up to run on the track in the early morning, at the same time as Shau Feng. Sometimes, in Shau Feng's company, he would express himself freely, but there were times when they were together that Paul acted withdrawn and appeared to be tongue-tied. Shau Feng would tilt her head and peer into his face and laugh.

"Paul, how do you expect me to expand my English vocabulary if you keep all the good words to yourself?" Shau Feng would lean over and walk beside him on her hands to cheer him up. On an occasion, Shau Feng scaled a lamppost to perform a handstand from the top brace. If Paul was in a playful mood and tried to touch her, Phoenix would pull away, explaining, "Paul don't take offense, but Chinese people don't like to have others put their hands on them." Shau Feng hoped Paul would believe this lame excuse, which was intended to protect her female identity.

One day, Shau Feng invited Paul to join her for lunch in the China House. He didn't answer right away, and so she pursued her invitation. "Paul, do you want to remain a frog in the well all your life?"

Paul shook his head. He said, "Give me time. I'm just learning to be comfortable with people."

"Paul, where were you reared, on a desert island? Weren't there any children in the schools you attended?"

Paul replied, "I'm off to the library. See you later."

Some young American women were openly flirting with Shau Feng. While the more aggressive ones asked Shau Feng for a date in front of Diana, others sent Shau Feng notes.

Paul teased Phoenix about the increasing number of young women showing up at football practice. He said, tongue-in-cheek, "A good-looking devil like you should have a stable of young women to demonstrate his prowess to. There are lots of beauties waiting on line to meet you. That redhead over there in the gray parka is dying to meet you." Eventually Shau Feng stopped Paul's teasing by yanking on his nose.

A close friendship existed among Phoenix, Paul, Robin, Casi, Jim, Harry, and Bronco, while they were just teammates to the other players. Casi and Jim were like brothers, bickering all the time over nothing. Robin was the jokester and was friends with all the guys. He entertained them with his talent for telling jokes. Harry and Bronco were cousins, who projected a rough-and-tumble cowboylike image. Everyone was aware of Casi, the macho

Latin lover, and his roving eyes. Many times from him they heard the words "I'm in love again; my body is on fire."

Paul walked down the street wrapped in his own thoughts. He was growing increasingly annoyed by the cluster of Chinese youths who surrounded Phoenix. They would speak to Phoenix in Chinese, which in a sense insulated his friend from him. He was finding it difficult to talk freely to Phoenix with so many people listening to their conversation. When he mentioned it, Phoenix replied, "They're just trying to protect me from being exposed to too much attention. They are also my friends, and they won't bite you." Phoenix loved to tease Paul about his shyness. "Why must you carry your shell everywhere you go? It's useless baggage." Paul's reaction was to go deeper into himself. Remembering that he called her a boy, she compared him to a blind man trying to describe an elephant, by touching a small section of the foot or the tail. The more time Paul spent in Phoenix's company, the more Phoenix baffled him.

He concluded Phoenix's odd behavior was due to their cultural differences. What had irked Shau Feng was Paul's constant harping about his early years spent feeling humiliated while attending school with holes in his pants. She would say that Paul's poor appearance had been created by the state of his outlook on life. When Paul said that his poverty was the result of being born into a poor family, Shau Feng replied, "While growing up, I didn't know what being born poor was like. But is there a law against a poor person becoming successful? Pretend to be rich; then you can also feel successful." Paul became uncomfortable with the subject. He couldn't respond. Murmuring something about being late for class, he fled.

Two days before football season began, Shau Feng received a call from her Aunt Sher Sher late in the night. Alarmed at the lateness of the call, Shau Feng waited for her aunt to explain the reason for the call. As gently as she could, Sher Sher informed Shau Feng that she was on her way to Hong Kong, because Lee Chen had suffered a stroke. The news shocked Shau Feng. She had only spoke to him the day before. She cried, "I want to go with you to see my grandfather."

Sher Sher braced herself and replied, "Father is being cared for by Dr. Ming at home, who told me that his condition wasn't life-threatening. It is more important for you to remain in school." There was a dead silence at the other end of the phone. Sher Sher prayed she had said the right thing to Shau Feng, who loved her grandfather very much. She hoped that Shau Feng would not get stubborn, which could become a problem.

Shau Feng was about to demand to go to Hong Kong, but a thought entered her mind. "Auntie must be feeling as bad as I am." In a subdued voice, she replied, "Auntie, I'll abide by your wish—although I want very much to go. I won't pressure you. I'm frightened—and my thoughts and prayers will be with Grandfather." Shau Feng's voice cracked, "Tell Grandfather that I love him." Something inside her head made her scream, "Tell him not to die!"

The words caused Sher Sher to tremble. She replied, "I shall, my dear. I'm sure he understands. Call me any time you wish at Father's house, in Hong Kong. Please don't hurt yourself Saturday in the game; otherwise your poor uncle would never forgive himself. Mr. Harris will be in touch with me about your progress. Good night, Shau Feng. Know that I will do everything possible within my power." So much was happening so fast that Shau Feng couldn't process it all. She would pray that night to Kwan Yi and ask for her help.

After Mrs. Nin Yee Kang had phoned Sher Sher to inform her that Master Chen had had a stroke, she decided to remain at the Chen residence and await Sher Sher's arrival. The old master's condition greatly distressed her. In all the years she had been with the Chen family, Mr. Chen had never been sick. As Nin Yee peered about the room, her thoughts gravitated toward the past. She cried softly, "Where have the years gone?"

Nin Yee rubbed her eyes and fingered the jade bracelet that Lavender, Master Chen's second wife, had given her on her deathbed. Since then, she had never removed it. Her mind went back to the time when Sher Sher was a child.

"Sher Sher was pretty, bright, imaginative, and had an excellent mind for detail, but she didn't have her mother's striking beauty. She never cared for housework or cooking; it was too routine for her. Somehow it was understood that I would care for the house. Master Chen brought Sher Sher to the theater with him while she was still a child. She certainly had a mind of her own, constantly questioning everyone about everything."

At the Chinese-Anglo Academy, Sher Sher was the brightest student they had ever had. She also had beaten up a few girls who had tried to bully her. Nin Yee recalled the day Sher Sher had graduated with honors. It had made her father very proud. It broke Master Chen's heart when Sher Sher married an American. He thought she was marrying beneath her. It wasn't much later that Master Chen retired from show business and opened his own actors' studio. The house and garden remained exactly as when Mrs. Chen was alive. And, from time to time, she would hear Master Chen talk to Lavender's picture. Just the thought of Lavender's spirit in the house was a source of great comfort to Mrs. Kang.

A taxi stopping at the front gate interrupted her musing. The housekeeper was on her feet with alacrity to open the gate. Sher Sher gave Mrs. Kang a hug and hastened to her father's room. In the bedroom, Sher Sher stared at her father's face, and tears swelled up in her eyes. Silently she started to cry. Her father had aged considerably since the last time she had seen him. The nurse seated by the bed told Sher Sher that Mr. Chen was only sleeping. Mrs. Kang stood by the door looking sad through puffy eyes. Before leaving her father's bedside, Sher Sher requested that the nurse call her if there were any change.

In her bedroom, Sher Sher found her suitcase had been

unpacked and her clothes put away. She changed into pajamas and went to the kitchen. In the hall, she heard Mrs. Kang talking, but, when she entered the kitchen there was no one else in the room. The housekeeper had been talking to Lavender's spirit while brewing tea. Sher Sher went into the living room for a bottle of brandy. She brought the bottle into the kitchen and poured two drinks. One, she handed to Mrs. Kang, and asked the good woman to share dinner with her. They ate in silence, each preoccupied with her own thoughts. That evening, Sher Sher meandered about the house that was still redolent with the scent of Lavender. Nothing had changed since her mother had died. On an impulse, she returned to her father's room. Sher Sher's sudden appearance startled the nurse, Miss Lin, who leaped out of the chair, causing the book she was reading to fall to the floor. She asked the nurse to go outside for some fresh air; she wanted to be alone with her father. Sher Sher studied her father's face while she stood beside the bed. He was still asleep. Very quietly Sher Sher took a chair and brought it to her father's bedside. She sat and took his cold hand in hers. Her restless eyes scanned the familiar room. There, on the far side of the wall, were pictures of herself as a child, and of Shau Feng in her academy uniform. The picture of her and Charles was nowhere in sight. Sher Sher's eyes returned to her father's face, and she compressed her lips to stifle a mournful sob. How she loved this old man. She sighed, "After all those years, Father still doesn't accept the fact I married an American." A strong squeeze of her hand made Sher Sher realize that her father's eyes were open.

Lee's face lit up as recognition came to him. Tears, like a river, flowed down Sher Sher's cheeks. Lee said in a weak voice, "Am I dreaming, or is it really you, My Child?"

"Yes, Father, it is I, your daughter."

The old man's voice gained in strength. "It seems like yesterday that I said good-bye at the airport."

"Father, excuse me or punish me for not being a more dutiful daughter."

Choking with passionate affection, he responded, "Daughter, you are better than this useless bag of old bones deserves." Nurse Lin tiptoed back into the room and softly announced that it was time for Master Chen's medicine.

Lee said, "Sher Sher, bring your ear to my mouth." She did. Lee whispered, "My will is located in the hidden place. Read it."

Nurse Lin went to her patient and gave Lee medicine. The nurse declared, "The doctor said that the master needs rest." Sher Sher nodded her head and left the room. Her father's eyes were closing.

After leaving her father's room, Sher Sher was on the phone, asking Dr. Ming for a report on her father's condition.

The doctor answered slowly, "It's not a matter of medication; it's his state of mind. It seems that his spirit has left him." Sher Sher screamed into the phone, "What are you saying, that my father is going to die?"

"Sher Sher, it depends on his will to live." It took Sher Sher a while to regain control of her emotions. The doctor asked, "Sher Sher, can I do anything for you?"

"No, I can handle it."

"How is Shau Feng?"

"Shau Feng is fine."

Late that evening, a much disturbed Sher Sher walked about the rear garden. Wind chimes hung from trees, and tinkled in the slightest breeze. Mrs. Kang brought tea. She placed the tray on a table and poured a cup. Sher Sher picked it up and thanked the woman. She saw the fatigue on the housekeeper's face and sent her to bed. Slowly Sher Sher sipped the hot tea, while her eyes focused on the water flowing out of the stone fish's mouth and dropping into a birdbath. She set the cup on the table, went to the center of the rear garden, and assumed a Tai Chi stance. Slowly raising her arms bit by bit, Sher Sher concentrated upon relaxation. She thought, "If Charles gets the impression from my voice that I need him, he will be on the next flight to Hong Kong. That must not happen; it would alarm Shau Feng." Sher Sher moved slowly, breathing in deeply the lavender-scented air, which acted like an elixir easing her troubled spirit.

It was very late in the night. After speaking to Charles on the phone, Sher Sher removed a box from its secret location in her old bedroom closet. She carried it to the desk. Inside the box, she found Shau Feng's horoscopes, her papers, Butterfly's letter to her father, her father's will, and, under that, her mother's jewel box. Inside the jewel box, on top of the jewelry, she found a sealed letter addressed to her, and, under the jewel box, she found a list of her father's business holdings. On the bottom were safe-deposit-box keys, and the names of the banks were taped to them. She opened her father's will. She was the major heir, with some of his assets going to Agile. Sher Sher returned the will to the box and opened the sealed letter addressed to her.

My dear child:
When you read this letter, you will already be an adult or your father will have passed away. I was the oldest of eight children, born into an extremely poor family. Saddled with frail health, I worked my way to graduate from high school. Believe me, my child, it wasn't easy. When my family was being ground to dust under the weight of poverty, the blessed God sent us an angel, your father. He gave us a new lease on life, unconditionally. I saw him as I hid in the next room. For me, it was love at first sight. I was determined to marry him. Our short time together was a blessing. You, my only child, are the fruit of our love. One's life span isn't measured in years, but in the way the time was used. Sher Sher, we had met numerous times in past lives; of this I'm certain. This time, I want to leave you with a gift to span time. I have given it much thought. Here it is: a mother's undying love.

Chen Lavender

Sher Sher refolded the letter and placed her palms on it. By this gesture, the daughter wanted to try to establish contact with the spirit of her late mother. She turned her head away from the letter, and tears fell, unchecked, down her cheeks. Sher Sher remained motionless for a long time at the desk. A current of air wrapped the lavender scent around her as dawn was breaking. The letter from her mother and the jewels were placed inside her suitcase. Everything else was returned to the box, which was replaced in the secret place.

In the morning, Sher Sher received her father's friends and business associates. She informed them that in the future she would handle all her father's affairs. Mr. Fong came in and brought flowers. He remained with her, talking, for hours. Hung Ma arrived among a group of students. Sher Sher took him aside to state that the acting school was now his. She didn't tell Hung Ma that the building housing the school would be his when her father passed away. When everyone had left, Sher Sher asked Mrs. Kang to join her for supper.

At the end of the second week that Sher Sher was in Hong Kong, her father recovered enough to walk with the aid of two canes. Insisting that he was feeling good and on his way to a full recovery, he requested that Sher Sher go home to Charles and Shau Feng. The day before Sher Sher departed, she called Shau Feng and handed the phone to her father. Lee told his granddaughter that he was feeling much better and not to worry. Sher Sher's father gave her a big hug before she left for the States. They looked at each other with love and affection in their eyes with a silent understanding that this would probably be for the last time. Sher Sher's last sight of her father was his smiling face.

8
Football Season

The night before the big football game was always a tense time for everyone on the team. Anxiety levels ran high, making a restful night's sleep almost impossible. Shau Feng was no exception. She tried to sleep, but her active mind kept her awake. Chet's parting words that evening had instilled within her a determination to win this football game. Also weighing heavily on her mind was her grandfather's condition. It wasn't until after midnight that she fell into a light and disturbed sleep. She dreamed that she was wrestling with faceless assassins, who emerged from a thick mist and attacked her from all sides. Shau Feng fought the vague apparitions, but her blows couldn't disable them. The dream broke up, and another appeared. She was dancing, with her head resting on a young man's shoulder. His arms about her were comforting. When she raised her head to look at his face, the dream ended. Shau Feng awoke with an overwhelming longing to go to Hong Kong to be at her grandfather's bedside, but she realized Aunt Sher Sher was right; there wasn't anything she could do for her grandfather but worry. Finally, at 4:15 A.M., Shau Feng rose, dressed, and left the China House for the track, hoping to release her agitation by running.

Outside the China House, a westerly breeze blew the fallen leaves from one side to another, mimicking the restlessness she felt. She arrived at the track and noticed that the benches had been freshly painted for today's game, and the wet-paint signs were still on the tier steps. Everything seemed to be in readiness, including Shau Feng.

Paul Armstrong's arms and legs spasmodically jerked in his sleep. He was having a perturbing dream. There in an obscure drama, he recognized Phoenix battling against shadowy foes. An overwhelming urge to help his friend possessed him. In that dream, Paul advanced across a field to help Phoenix, but was confronted with a deep and wide chasm. Frustration flooded his mind as his body rolled around in bed. An outpouring of adrenaline surged through him, for he was determined to leap across the chasm. Paul raced forward and jumped into the air. He awoke on his feet, sweating and breathing laboriously in the cold room. It was hard to shake off the dream; it had seemed so real. Paul dressed hurriedly and left the Caruso House. The cold air stung his face and shocked him awake. Paul walked to the football field, attempting to clench his fists. Feeling something in his right hand, his eyes went to it. He was amazed to discover that he was carrying a football.

Paul didn't expect to see anyone on the field at this hour, but a fleeting moving figure on the track caught his eye. A smile came on Paul's face, his entire body relaxed as he recognized his friend Phoenix. When the runner emerged from the darkness into a lighted area, Paul threw the ball toward him and shouted, "Heads up and look alive, Shrimp!" Instinctively Shau Feng caught the ball and tossed it back to him. She leaned into a handstand. Paul came and said, "How does the world look upside down?"

"It sharpens one's perspective. You ought to try it sometime." Walking on her hands, she uprighted herself right in front of him.

"Give me an easy five, buddy," said Paul, "and save some of your energy for Columbus." The contact with Phoenix's hand brought a grin to his face. Wordlessly they walked off the track to Main St. "Phoenix, join me for breakfast?"

"Okay."

At the eastern horizon, the sun gave indication that it was rising. It was still cold with a mild wind that blew in from the west.

Shau Feng was escorted to the football field by the coach's wife, Mrs. Harris. They were joined by a group of Chinese students: Rachel, Edith, tall Terry, short Terry and Judy. They were there to see the Lions play and to give their friend moral support, should it be needed.

Coach Harris eyed the eager faces of the players and declared, "Men, play as you have been taught, and I'll take you all the way to the championship game—that is a promise. You have what it takes to earn those rings." As the players went to the benches, Chet said, under his breath, "God bless you all."

Then Joe said, "Lions, remember: no guts, no glory. Let's show those guys out there we came to play football and win."

As team captain, Silent Sam, a tall, husky rawboned young man, trotted out to the field for the toss. Columbus won the toss and elected to receive the ball. They got the ball and went nowhere. They kicked it away. Brown took Robin and Phoenix by the arm and said, "Birds, fly for the Lions today. You can burn these dudes with your speed. Teach Columbus to respect us." Off they went into the huddle. Brown figured the first time Phoenix sped past them, they would double-team Phoenix or try to take him out of the game. That's what he would have told his people to do if he had been on the other side. Paul was given the number of the play. Phoenix yelled, "All for me!" then slapped her teammates' hands. They replied, "One for all!"

After the ball was snapped, Paul stepped into the pocket, and three Lions receivers raced into the Columbus Bears' backfield. The safeties converged to cover them. Being well protected, Paul waited, seeking an open receiver.

All the Bears' safeties had been briefed about Robin's speed. Stretch, the tallest player for the Lion, six-six, was on Paul's left, being covered. Robin outlegged Phoenix, who was some yards behind him. When he cut to the right, Phoenix continued to run, but at the Bears' safety, converging on Robin. The broad-shouldered football player dug his toes into the ground as he ran, believing that Phoenix would attempt to slow him down with a block. Before the collision, Shau Feng sidestepped the safety. Increasing her speed, she raced out in the open, and up came her hands. Paul saw Phoenix in the open and threw the ball right into her hands. She increased her pace and outdistanced the other safeties cutting across the field to intercept her. It was too late. The Bears couldn't catch Phoenix. The touchdown brought the audience out of their seats, shouting wildly. Chet removed his cap and waved it in the air. The bet with the Bears coach on the outcome of the game was for a bottle of champagne. Joe and Wilton clapped their hands in approval.

It was the second play for the Lions that broke the back of the Bears' game plan. A quick pass for short yardage was thrown to Phoenix, who was double-covered. Instead of running out of bounds, she raced between the safeties for open space. This unexpected move caught her tacklers off guard. With a display of broken field running and speed, Shau Feng scored for a second time.

Paul had been blitzed several times. Chet was impressed with the young man's reaction. The Chinese were on their feet, yelling and waving banners. Chet smiled. Both assistant coaches, like old warriors, felt a victory in the wind. Phoenix was benched for the rest of the game. Joe wanted to see what the others could do in this game. Shau Feng's energy level was up. She paced the sidelines, shouting encouragement to her teammates. It was then that Shau Feng had the chance to observe Paul in action.

It appeared to her that Paul was unruffled and poised under attack, and she dubbed him "Mr. Cool." At half-time, the score was 20–0. During the third quarter, Bronco and Harry's running game chewed up the clock. Bronco burst through the Bears' line for a touchdown. The Columbus team was badly outclassed. Chet was walking among his players and whistling. Joe Wilton had given everyone a chance to play that day, and they had come through like champions. All hell broke loose on the field when the game was over. Dr. Oriello, seated among the alumni, received their congratulations. For Plainfield College, this was their first home winning game in five years. The student body was intoxicated with the win. Shau Feng was swamped on the field by the exhilarated Chinese. Under Chet's direction, they marched Shau Feng off the field, singing as they returned to the China House. After noting that Shau Feng was in safe hands, Chet allowed himself to be carried around the track on the shoulders of the male cheerleaders.

When Jo-An wanted to join Shau Feng, she passed Bronco walking with Harry. The young men stared at her, their faces breaking into smiles, which annoyed Jo-An. She defensively yelled, "What are you staring at—Jerk?" and ran as fast as she could into the group of Chinese students massed around Shau Feng. Robin and Paul came to Bronco and Harry. They congratulated each other. Harry slapped Paul on the back and said, "Great job, Mr. Cool."

Paul asked, "Where did I get that name from?"

Harry replied, "Phoenix gave it to you."

Paul said, "Now I know why they call you Harry the Horse. You charge your way through anything."

He pointed to Bronco. "My cousin said I act more like a jackass than a horse."

Robin said, "Did you hear what Phoenix said to the guys? He thanked us for the honor and privilege of playing with us. The shrimp piled the credit on us all." Robin replied, as they started to walk, "Phoenix is a rare bird. I would say, one of a kind. There is no doubt about how fast he can run. Besides, the Dutchman, his uncle, taught him how to play football."

Bronco added, "Maybe we should give him the credit."

Casi and Jim were surrounded by young women. A woman was interviewing them for an article for the college newspaper, when Paul came to them. He asked, "Jim, are you coming with us?"

"Yes, I'm coming, but now I'm doing business with my public. Wasn't I great?"

"Jim, there is nobody else like you on the team."

"Paul, you certainly know how to call your plays." They both laughed. "See if you can get the shrimp to come with us into town tonight."

In the China House, after gathering her laundry, Shau Feng went to the basement. Upon returning to her room, she found that the red light on the answering machine was blinking. She immediately thought, "Something has happened to Grandfather." She ran to depress the answering machine's 'play' button. It was Paul's voice, asking her to join some guys in town tonight at 7:00 P.M. He added that the goons would throw him through the window of the China House's front door if Phoenix refused.

"Save my life, Little Shrimp." The remark brought a smile to her face. Shau Feng thought that Paul could often be funny, although most times he took himself too seriously. She returned the call, asking him to meet her in the China House at 6:00 P.M. that night.

Paul showered, shaved, combed his hair, and dressed in his best clothes. He was pleased with himself for being clever enough to extract Phoenix from the protective clutches of the Chinese. It bothered Paul that the Chinese always spoke their native language to Phoenix in front of him. Paul lived in a small room on the third floor in the Caruso House. He mentally counted his tightly budgeted money. There was enough for one blowout a month. In his mind, he wondered if it were normal to like a person of one's own sex. He thought that Phoenix, who smelled of lavender scent, might be a homosexual. It passed lightly through his mind, but he dismissed it immediately. Phoenix hung around with too many young women at the China House to fit the image. The young Chinese men treated Phoenix with respect. He was confused, didn't know what to make of it, and decided to erase it from his mind for the time being.

It was 6:00 P.M. Paul was outside the front door to the China House, waiting for Phoenix. He stood with his back toward the door. Shau Feng came out like a hurricane, deliberately running into him and knocking him forward a few steps. Paul yelled, "Hey, remember me? I'm on your side. Where are you flying to today?"

Feeling in a playful mood, she grinned at him and replied, "Paul, it's cold outside. Why didn't you come inside, where it's warm, as I asked you to do?" He looked at his feet.

"Those people who live in there don't like me. They speak only Chinese whenever I'm around and exclude me from their conversations. Sometimes I think they are talking about me. Some of them look at me cross-eyed."

Stunned, Shau Feng said, "Stop being so sensitive. You Americans say things in front of me that I don't understand, and nobody bothers to translate or explain them to me. People speak in whatever language they feel comfortable. If you are looking for sympathy, you came to the wrong person. Why should you imagine things that aren't so?" Paul's face turned red. He tried to walk away. Shau Feng restrained him by grabbing the back of his jacket.

"Paul, tell me what's wrong. I didn't mean to hurt you. Even though we come from different cultures, can't we still be friends? I'm willing to meet you halfway, and here's my hand on it. Will you accept it?"

Paul averted Phoenix's face. His friend had touched upon a sore spot. How could he explain to Phoenix his innermost fears? Paul mumbled a halfhearted excuse. "My pride is all I have, and I guess sometimes it gets in the way, but it's not easy for me to get over the fear of being rejected. Let's go. The others are waiting for us."

After the late movie, five Plainfield football players entered the Roma Restaurant. During the meal, Robin teased Casi and Jim over the amount of food they were consuming. He said they ate enough food to feed an army. Robin told a joke about French soldiers who traveled on their stomachs. Paul remarked, "These two could travel hundreds of miles on what they consumed."

Shau Feng said, "It would be cheaper to clothe them than feed them."

Unruffled, they replied, "We earned our keep on the football field today. Didn't we prevent that mountain of humanity from flattening our little Shrimp? Squirt, that big guy would have turned you into a pancake." Jim reached for the last piece of garlic bread, stuffing it in his mouth. Suddenly Casi clutched his stomach and arose, running for the nearest toilet.

Jim gleefully said, "He's got the curse of the Alamo." All broke into hilarious laughter, except Shau Feng.

Noting the blank look on Phoenix's face, Paul said, "You don't get it, do you?" Shau Feng shook her head. Paul explained that the remark referred to the Texans' version of "Montezuma's Revenge," which was diarrhea, but Shau Feng thought that a discussion of bodily functions wasn't proper conversation at a dinner table. She suggested to Paul that it was time to leave.

Having missed the last bus to the college because of Casi's long stay in the toilet, they had to walk to the campus. While on the darkened road, Paul asked Phoenix to teach him some useful Chinese words. Before Shau Feng could reply, a police cruiser came along and stopped next to the walkers. After the youths identified themselves, Sheriff Lawrence Johnson gave them a lift back to college, which was just what they needed. Since they were all crowded in the back of the cruiser, Paul discontinued the Chinese lesson with Phoenix. He didn't want the others to get the wrong idea and tease him. For Phoenix, it was a time for quiet and reflection. Her grandfather was on her mind.

It had been a week since Sher Sher returned from Hong Kong. After dinner, Sher Sher and Charles took a walk around their estate. The dog, Shau De, following closely at his mistress' heels.

The night was brilliant. Fiery stars appeared like cold diamonds in the inky sky. Wind gusts pushed against their bodies as they sauntered along the paved path. Sher Sher slipped her gloved hand on her husband's arm. Charles was glad to have her back home. He had missed her while she was away. During the last week, Charles had noticed a change in Sher Sher. There was an aura of inner calm about her. They stopped to look at a shooting star. Charles, studying Sher Sher's face, saw that there was sadness in her eyes.

"What's on your mind, Old Girl? Are you still worried about your father?" Her gaze went across the sky. He said, "Love, we have more money than we can spend in a lifetime. Let's travel around the world." Sher Sher gave him a tender look. Gently she raised her gloved hand to caress his face and said, "Darling, I want Mrs. Kang to have Mother's house, should Father die."

"I see no problem."

"Charles, I want to adopt Shau Feng as our daughter, in the Chinese way."

"Fine with me. I already love her like a daughter." And they continued on their walk, hand in hand. Shau De brushed against Sher Sher's knee. She touched the dog's head, and the dog kissed her gloved hand. From her pocket, Sher Sher removed a thick golden chain with a jade Buddha. Charles looked at what was in her gloved hand, while she extended the chain to him.

"Father wants you to have his lucky charm. It was given to him by a monk on the day he fled China."

Charles felt uncomfortable and didn't reach for it, because he was aware Lee had never liked him. The big man replied, "I don't need a lucky charm. I've got you."

Sher Sher arched an eyebrow. "I want you to wear Father's lucky piece!" Charles looked away from her. "Are you listening to me?" The last sentence was in Chinese. He thought that it was better not to argue with her.

"Yes, I will accept it with the hope that he lives a long time."

A mock blow from Sher Sher touched his arm, and she

grabbed him by the coat. "Do you know I love you, you big ox? Put it around your neck. The Hong Kong goldsmith who enlarged the chain thought it was for a horse." Suddenly Shau De darted after a rabbit. Sher Sher felt the dog brush past her. She called the dog back. Sher Sher shook a finger at the dog. "How many times have I told you to leave the rabbits alone?" The dog leaned forwards to bite her glove playfully.

Charles jokingly said, "Let's give the mutt away. He only eats, sleeps all day, and sheds hair over the house. Some watchdog—he would kiss any burglar who broke into our house."

Sher Sher cried out, "Are you crazy? The first things that would be given away are your dust-collecting trophies." She twisted her mouth, and he playfully kissed it, which was a signal to stop the bickering.

Charles's mind had focused a painful memory as they walked. In his mind came pictures of his three friends who had played professional football on the same team with him. It had happened the night they were returning from Gloria's birthday party. If not for that accident, his friend Eric and Gloria would have been engaged and married. The road surface was slick from the recent rain. Eric had stopped the car at a traffic light. A heavily loaded truck had come from behind and tried to stop, but skidded into the rear of their car, killing his two friends and leaving him with a back injury.

Recurring nightmares about the accident filled Charles's dreams. He was constantly being caught in quicksand, unable to reach his friends, who were sinking, one by one, beneath the sand. Time passed, and his back injury healed, but it disabled him and kept him from playing in a professional league. It was that same year that Charles was voted into the Football Hall of Fame. An ironclad contract and a lucrative insurance policy made him rich, but the loss of his football career and the death of his friends had caused a deep depression.

After he left the hospital, Charles had locked himself in his apartment for days, not seeing anyone, not even his mother. The young giant would stare for hours at his hands and do nothing but cry. All offers to coach football teams were refused. He had no heart to see anyone of the old crowd.

For three months, Charles had lived like a hermit in his apartment. Finally, one day, he went out for an aimless stroll. After hours and miles of walking, Charles felt hunger pains and had gone into a Chinese restaurant in the San Francisco Bay area. He had seated himself near a table near where four young women were loudly laughing. They were there to celebrate their graduation from college. The sound of their happy voices drew Charles's attention to them. A pretty Chinese woman, feeling eyes upon her, turned to look at him. He smiled at her. She smiled back and beckoned him to join them. Charles reluctantly walked to the women's table, not knowing what would happen. The young Chinese woman explained the reason for the celebration and asked him to join them. Charles agreed. As Sher Sher talked, there was an immediate attraction between the two of them. Six weeks later, after a whirlwind courtship, they were married. He came out of his reverie, hearing Sher Sher's voice.

"You've been silent too long. What were you thinking about?" His reply was quick, accompanied by a big hug.

"I was thinking how glad I am to be your husband."

It was after 8:00 P.M., and Paul was outside the closed library building, cursing himself for having forgotten to wear his hat or gloves. The wind was blowing briskly, and the weather had turned raw, yet he didn't want to go back for his hat or gloves. Paul stood on the top step of the library against the door, keeping out of the wind, while he waited for Phoenix. This was the Lions' fourth victory in a row. He had called his friend Phoenix, who had agreed to meet him at the library, and suggested they take a short walk before getting something to eat. Two young men, carrying a boom box, came hurriedly down the street bundled against the cold. They recognized their football hero rubbing his hands together and shouted, "Hi, Mr. Cool! We whipped the ass off Brunswick today!"

Paul replied, "We were lucky," and continued on. Paul removed all the coins in his pockets and recounted them. There was enough to buy a slice of pizza and a small Coke. He shifted from foot to foot while putting his hands against his bare body to keep them warm. Paul straightened up as he spied Phoenix coming fast along the street.

"Doesn't the kid ever relax? Where does he get that energy? I'm wiped out from today's game." A few feet from Paul, Phoenix came to a stop. Paul noticed his friend was all bundled up, but still wore that silly hat pulled over his ears. Paul found he was staring into Phoenix's eyes a bit longer than usual. This made him uncomfortable.

Shau Feng looked at bareheaded and gloveless Paul and thought that he must be well insulated against the cold.

"Hi, Paul."

"Hi, Phoenix. Wasn't it a good game today?"

"Yes, I thought it was fun." They moved on, discussing the next game and reviewing the last one. When they came to where Birch St. met Main St., Phoenix realized that it was too cold to be outdoors, because Paul was shivering in his Lions jacket. She didn't want this dummy to get frostbite or catch cold. Tabard was a few blocks away.

"Let's go to Tabard, okay?" Paul nodded okay.

She said, "I'm feeling lucky after all our wins. Paul, would you get upset if I paid the check as a treat?"

Paul stiffened and appeared aloof. His voice took on a sharp edge. "Yes, I would! Look, Kid, I know your family is wealthy. Your pocket money for a week could be more than I earn in a month working at the cafeteria. I prefer to pay my own way." Shau Feng's nostril's flared, and she stamped her foot in the cold ground.

"Paul, when you work, the money you receive is yours. You earned it. Besides, my parents are far from being rich! Without the generosity of my grandfather and my aunt and uncle, I would be penniless. It's their money in my pocket! What is wrong if I want to share some of my good fortune with a friend? A free meal or two wouldn't damage your bloated pride. I thought we were friends." Shau Feng backed away from Paul. "It's a mistake for me to be here. I try to understand you, but sometimes you make it difficult. I'm going back to the China House. Good-bye!"

Phoenix's words bit deeply into Paul. The resentment on his friend's face stung him. In Paul's mind, he knew Phoenix was right. The shock and realization of being about to lose his good friend forced him to retreat. Paul took a few steps toward Phoenix. Trembling, he said, "Phoenix, don't leave."

The anger swelling inside caused Phoenix not to notice the pain on Paul's face. She blurted out, "Why should I stay with someone who rejects friendship? All I hear from you is 'my pride'!"

Wretchedness was written all over Paul's face. He said, in a hoarse voice, "You started it."

"Did I? People treat me all the time, and offer me companionship. I don't reject it as you do!"

Shau Feng cast her eyes down, saw a small stone near her shoe, and kicked it. She barely recognized Paul's voice, when he said, "Phoenix, please forgive me for offending you. My poverty hangs heavy on me. I know it's a stupid excuse. Please don't leave. You are the only friend I ever had." His voice broke, trailing off into silence. Shau Feng's temper subsided.

"Paul, I'm a stranger here." Her eyes went to his face. "I too have pride. Keeping face is very important to Asians. It's the same thing as your pride. I may speak your language, but I am Chinese. I don't wish to hurt you. Let's try to understand each other better, okay?"

Paul made a complete circle, standing on one foot, then bowed from the waist. "Phoenix, I accept your treat as a bridge to mutual understanding and respect for each other's feelings. Shall we go to Tabard?"

Shau Feng replied, "Paul, I'll laugh with you, not at you, if you promise to keep your burdensome pride in check and not let it get the best of you." They shook hands.

"Last one to reach Tabard's eats slime balls," declared Paul, and off he ran, down Main St.

"Ugh! How gross."

Paul raced along the street, heading for the restaurant. Shau Feng was covering a zigzag course, leaping over benches, trailing him. Paul passed a lamppost, where Phoenix won a bet, climbing it and performing a one-handed handstand more than once. He had asked Phoenix where his energy had come from. The kid said that it came from Chinese food. How he wished he had some Chinese food inside him right now! Tabard's was a few yards ahead, and Paul's legs felt like lead. He ceased running and bent over to catch his breath. Paul looked around for Phoenix. The kid was a foot away, laughing. Even though Paul's chest ached from the strain of running, feeling relieved, he broke into a laugh. He finally caught his breath and said, "Shame on you for throwing the race." Shau Feng covered her mouth, suppressing a giggle. Without thinking, Paul held the door open to Tabard's.

Inside the restaurant, the warm air hit them immediately, causing sweat to pour down from their bodies. The place was constructed like a rectangle, with booths lining both sides of the walls. Paul saw a vacant booth, and Phoenix followed him to it. They slid into the booth, peeling off their coats. Shau Feng wore an extra-large, shapeless red sweater that Uncle Charles had brought for her. Paul wore a yellow-and-blue thermal vest over a faded blue shirt. They glanced around the room, settling down. Across the room by the counter, nursing a soft drink, sat Jim, alone. Brian and David were at a table near the center of the room, with two girls. Shau Feng asked Paul to invite Jim over to join them.

Paul came over to Jim. "Hi, Jim."

"Hi, yourself."

"Jim, Phoenix wants to treat you to some pizza."

Jim replied, "It would be a pleasure." Paul mentioned the tiff with Phoenix that had resulted in their both losing their tempers.

Jim brought his face inches away from Paul. "You are a klutz. One socializes over a meal, which is a naturally accepted means of communication by most people in the civilized world. Sure, Phoenix has a temper, but so do you! Do you have any idea who the Lemars are?"

"Sure, Charles Lemar is the husband of Phoenix's aunt and also a retired football great."

"Paul, my boy, throw away your one-donkey concept of the world. Phoenix acts odd because you measure him with your ruler. Open your closed mind to allow in some insight into your world. Enough of this gas, I'm hungry. Let's go and eat."

Jim greeted Phoenix and slid into the semicircular booth beside her. With a smile, she said, "Jim, for your outstanding performance on the field, please feel free to order anything you like. This treat is on me."

Jim clasped his hands together. "Thank you, Phoenix. It's a rare thing for one to have my natural talent appreciated." He opened the menu, said, "Oh, me, oh, my, a second blessing on you, Little Shrimp." Jim crossed himself, looking upward. "Oh, Lord, if I'm dead or dreaming, don't awaken me until after I finish this meal."

Paul said, "What kind of praying is that?"

"Paul, we are in mixed company, so don't show your backward breeding. Son, loosen your head, because it's screwed on too tight."

The waitress came to take their order. "What will it be today?"

Jim said, rubbing his hands together, "I'll start off with an extra-large platter of fettucine al Fredo, a dozen raw fresh clams on the half-shell, a loaf of garlic bread. . . . "

Paul placed his hand over Jim's mouth. He spoke to the waitress. "Sorry, he is delirious. Don't listen to him."

Shau Feng said, "I'll order. A kitchen-sink pizza, a large pizza with extra cheese and meatballs, and three large Cokes."

Jim protested, "Phoenix, old buddy, I'll starve on that skimpy diet. I'm a growing boy."

Paul replied, "True, Baby Jim is still growing, but sideways."

They discussed the upcoming game, which would be played away from home, in Denver, the following week. When the food arrived, Jim picked up a slice and blew on it. He tucked over the sagging end and took a bite. Paul reached for a slice of pie. From the corner of his eye, he noticed Phoenix squirming in the seat. He said, "Dig in, before the monster eats it all."

She recoiled. "Is there anything wrong?"

"I don't know how to eat pizza with my hands."

"Act like an American. This is finger food." Shau Feng put a slice on a paper plate. Jim dominated the conversation while they ate. His wit, sharp mind, and glib tongue made him friends as well as enemies.

From the other side of the room came a young redheaded woman, who stopped by Shau Feng's table. She smiled broadly at Phoenix, then at Paul. The perfume she wore seemed to radiate from her body. Rita placed her palms against the tabletop, bending from the waist, looked directly at Phoenix, then Paul. The low-cut dress almost entirely exposed her well-shaped breasts to their view. The young men's eyes drank in the splendor they saw. Shau Feng froze in the seat, staring up at Rita in disbelief.

"My name is Rita Hastings." Her tongue came out of her mouth, wetting lipstick-covered lips. The woman's eyes reached out at Phoenix in attempt to read his reaction. Rita overpraised Phoenix and Paul's athletic abilities, while Jim grinned from ear to ear. He interjected that he was the team's spark plug and playmaker. But Rita's eyes were only for Phoenix and Paul. Jim's eyes watched the ample breasts and Rita's swaying of her body. She blew Phoenix a kiss, then invited him to party with her in the future. Since Phoenix didn't reply, she stood erect and slowly walked away.

Jim said, "Have a nice day, Rita!"

"Knock it off." Jim and Paul couldn't help but feel amused by this turn of events. Shau Feng's face was scarlet. Her mouth hung open. Paul, upon seeing Phoenix's reaction to Rita's come-on invitation, lightly kicked Jim under the table with his foot and directed his eyes toward Phoenix. They winked at each other. Paul said, "Jim, old buddy, did you notice what color Rita's toenails were?"

"Toenails? You did say toenails, didn't you? Why, of course, I saw them while looking down past her breasts. They were misty red." Rita's behavior had made Shau Feng uncomfortable. She was not used to overt sexual behavior between men and women. Paul touched Phoenix's arm and, speaking in a low voice, told her, "Play it cool, Little Shrimp, no laughing. Just raise your head and smile. Act cosmopolitan, making like this happens to you all the time. We don't want to lose face among our American classmates. Rita was just acting friendly in her own way." They loudly laughed until their sides ached. Shau Feng saw that the young men were teasing her. All of a sudden, she felt sick and tired of playing the male role.

The trio filled the empty platters with their soiled napkins. Appearing pleased with the food, Jim rubbed his stomach. Shau Feng caught the waitress's eye, asking for the check. "It's time for me to leave," she said. Jim and Paul thanked Phoenix for the treat. Paul slid out of the booth, and Phoenix came after him. She put on her coat, hat, and gloves. Paul and Jim wanted to stay there and talk to Silent Sam, who had just come in minutes earlier.

Shau Feng declared, "I don't think I'll ever forget this night. Bye."

"Good night, Phoenix." Now Jim and Paul's attention went to Brian and David's table.

Jim thought, "I'll destroy the pricks if they follow Phoenix out the door."

Paul said, "I'll rearrange their faces if they follow Phoenix."

Jim questioned Paul, "Redneck, can you read minds?"

"No, why do you ask such a question?"

"Skip it. Did you notice that the shrimp ate like a bird? Do you think that Phoenix didn't care for the food? I read somewhere that Asians don't eat cheese."

"Phoenix ate some, didn't he?"

"That proves he has better manners than you, Plowboy."

"Am I that bad?"

"Ask yourself that question, not me. Just look at Rita. She has the hots for our friend. She is looking for a trophy football player for a boyfriend. Phoenix doesn't need Rita. That handsome Chinese doesn't react to women the way we do. He has class, something you lack. As for women, a long line of pretty Chinese faces are after him. Poor guy—doesn't know what he's in for."

It was the last Sunday of October. After breakfast, the Chinese gathered in the reception room, in the China House, for a meeting. Only residents of the China House attended this gathering, so Mrs. Chou was not present. Carl Ho reported that the abusive behavior of the Americans toward the Chinese at this college was at an all-time low. He credited that to Shau Feng's fists and heroic action. Several factions began speaking at the same time. A few Chinese were not enthusiastic about Shau Feng playing football on a boys' team. The majority let it be known they would fix anyone who betrayed their heroine.

Shau Feng stood up, and asked for everyone's attention. First she described what had transpired at Tabard's the night before with Rita Hastings, and then she said, "Due to the fact that I must act like a young man, some young women push themselves at me. They give me funny looks. I don't know how to handle it. Please help me." Jo-An contorted her mouth in disapproval and was about to rise to say something.

Rachel, seated next to her, cautioned Jo-An to hold her tongue, and whispered, "Don't speak when you are angry. Let's hear what the others have to say first, okay?" Edith knew that name-calling wasn't the solution, because all women did not act like Rita.

Bruce Tong, who was known as a deep thinker and not an accomplished speaker, stood up. The thick glasses he wore made his eyes appear very large. It was evident that Shau Feng needed help. He addressed the meeting. "Brothers and sisters of China, we must protect Shau Feng. She plays football not for personal glory, but for the honor of the Chinese. We must not turn our backs on her. As a group, we must plan how to accomplish this task. The fallout of Shau Feng's success on the football field will result in her being in the public spotlight. Therefore, we must never, ever, let down our vigil. If we fail in this task, we fail our own countrymen." Bruce paused and strolled among the students, looking directly into everyone's face. At the beginning, he spoke in a very low voice, working his way to a normal tone. "As Shau Feng becomes well known to the public, hoardes of newspaper reporters will descend upon this college. Some will speak our language. They might ask searching questions about Phoenix's background. What shall we tell them? Will there be different stories to arouse their curiosity? A red herring must be created to mislead the public from discovering Shau Feng's true identity. We shall counter any fight story on the campus with disinformation techniques, to confuse the reporters. They are the troublemakers. These news-media people, with their innocent questions and tape recorders, aren't fools." He suddenly shouted, "Among us, who will disgrace Shau Feng in front of the Americans?" The walls vibrated with the power of his voice. It had its effect. These waiting young Chinese faces shouted that they would back Shau Feng. All eyes were upon him for direction.

Bruce gazed a second time at Shau Feng. He asked himself, "Shau Feng, which god looks after you? Did some great power send you to change our lives and invigorate our weakened souls?" Bruce raised his arms above his head. "We of the Chinese nation will tell the world that Phoenix Chen learned his football from his uncle, Mr. Charles Lemar, a hall-of-fame football player. Coach Chet Harris will be pushed into the limelight. Neither he nor anyone will ever reveal where Shau Feng came from. We shall shrug our shoulders when asked such questions." Bruce's voice lowered to a conspiratorial whisper. "Brothers and sisters, I repeat, we must hide Shau Feng's martial skill from the public. Declare all Phoenix's fights on the campus as never having happened. Laughingly, we shall say, they were elaborate gags."

Short and emaciated-looking to the point where his ribs showed, Bruce Tong's only loves were books. He thirsted for the knowledge that enabled him to rise above others. Bruce rationalized that his parents, teachers, classmates, and the people around him didn't understand him, and he was sensitive to criticism. It injured his pride when the mirror revealed that he was short and plain looking. In his mind's eye, Bruce created a picture of himself. The one he conceived was intelligent, brave, benevolent, and resourceful. The youth would condescend to do his duty to his parents by marrying and having children, but, at this stage in his young life, he didn't care much for women. Women annoyed and puzzled him. He was unhappy in his current life and had been weighted down by a sense of helplessness, until Shau Feng had burst upon the scene like a hero of old times. Her character, like a cleansing wind, had blown away the lethargy clinging to him. The young woman's agreement to teach him Kung-Fu had invigorated his oppressed soul. Daily, he practiced what she taught him, with the same drive and passion that made him a top student. Revenge against the Americans who had picked on him was foremost on his mind, but, through his contact with Shau Feng, that had melted away, and Bruce had learned forgiveness. Shau Feng had opened his eyes by displaying, in the face of danger, strength and courage.

Bruce returned to the China House late that afternoon, just in time to receive a phone call from Coach Harris. Knowing that Bruce was a computer hack, he wanted to enlist Bruce's help in changing Shau Feng's records. Bruce thanked the coach and agreed readily, only too happy to be of service to Shau Feng. It was a quiet time at the China House, a time of day when everyone was off, doing his or her thing. Being a computer hacker at heart, he had no problem accessing the college's computer. He alerted Shau Feng's records by deleting all references to her being female. He inserted a medical history using the name of his uncle, who was a doctor.

After he had completed the change of Shau Feng's records, Bruce inserted a diskette on chess inside the PC. His fingers flew over the keyboard. On the monitor appeared a chess game. This time he would select the white. As he gazed at the screen, his mind was not on the game. It bothered him that Paul was hanging out with Shau Feng. In his mind, Shau Feng was too good to be wasting her time with that useless fellow. Even though he realized Paul thought Shau Feng was a male, he was thinking about the future. "What a mess!" Bruce forced his mind to stay on the chess game.

The Plainfield Lions were the most talked about team in college football broadcasting. Film clips of their games appeared on the sports segments of the TV news. Chet's past record was reprinted in newspapers and commented on, on television, on radio, to refresh the readers' minds. The Lions' winning record became a feature story. The sportscasters and writers dubbed the Lions "the Cinderella team of the year." Serious sportsmen didn't believe that the Lions had a chance to defeat the mighty Eagles, because the Eagles were the best college football team in the past ten years. Now Paul, Bronco, Silent Sam, Harry, Robin, and Phoenix became household names. Phoenix Chen was rated the fastest runner in the college circuit. The Lions' win made Plainfield, Ohio, seem much larger than just a dot on the map.

Plainfield's Chamber of Commerce planned their celebration to coincide with that of the college's yearly open house. It was to take place on the weekend before Thanksgiving. Due to that extensive media coverage and the expected influx of people, the state police were asked to help with policing the town. A flood of requests arrived from eager people who wanted to see and be seen at the open house. The college's facilities and those of the town were unable to satisfy their requests. The problem was given over to campus security.

Sheriff Johnson deputized a hundred local citizens to help direct traffic. Signs went up, making the town streets off limits to all vehicles. Special buses were rented by the town to transport people coming by bus and train to the college. Those arriving by automobile were directed to the local airport, which was utilized as a parking lot. The mayor of Plainfield officially asked the state police for assistance. In the town, souvenirs of the Lion team were sold everywhere. The Lions' winning streak created a festive atmosphere, as the town hired roving bands to entertain their guests. The photographers did a land-office business selling pictures of the customer's head inserted in a Lions' football player's cutout.

Saturday afternoon, the China House was filled with people. Dr. Oriello, Chet's wife's sister, was among the welcoming committee at the basketball courts, which had been converted into a reception hall. Mr. and Mrs. Harris, Mr. and Mrs. Brown and Mr. and Mrs. Claymore also shared the honor of hosting the event. Mr. and Mrs. Lemar were among the visitors at the China House.

Among the people called upon to entertain the guests were local bush-league performers and in-house talent. There was an announcement taped on the front door of the China House. It said that Phoenix Chen would perform an episode from *The Monkey King*. It also said that Gene Hu would play the piano, accompanied by Sara, Amanda, and Diana, on guitars. Meanwhile, Bruce Tong was in the kitchen, putting together his props for his magic act.

Upstairs, Shau Feng was seated, while her aunt Sher Sher applied makeup to her face. The young woman was excited and couldn't sit still. Sher Sher had to tap her on the head to get her to stop moving around. Downstairs, catered food was being served. Mrs. Chou coordinated the operation and gave orders that nobody was to be allowed upstairs other than the resident students.

Shau Feng entered the reception hall searching the faces of the audience for Paul. She couldn't locate him. During the past three weeks, Paul had begun to distant himself from her. He was irritable, impolite, impersonal at practice, and he generally shied away from her. Brenda mentioned to Shau Feng that Paul was seeing Rita Hastings. Mr. Cool and Miss Hot-Pants had become an item on the campus. Shau Feng felt a pang of jealousy at Paul's attention to Rita, but she realized that, after all, Paul thought of her as a man, not as the woman she was. Yet that still didn't completely explain what had suddenly come over Paul, causing him to withdraw from her, even though she knew the relationship was complicated. She didn't even understand her own feeling toward him.

Paul arrived at the China House in time to catch the end of Phoenix's performance on stage and see Charles Lemar swelling with pride, handing Phoenix yellow roses. Paul was in awe of Phoenix's many talents. What had bothered him was that recently Phoenix appeared different to him each time he saw him. It was positively schizophrenic; it was as if his eyes were a kaleidoscope, seeing Phoenix as a male one time and a female at another time. Lately, it seemed he was beginning steadily to perceive Phoenix as a female. Paul couldn't understand what had happened to him. He remembered, from Psych 1, that it took some adolescents a longer time than others to develop sexual identity, and that sometimes they turned to their own sex for affection. But it seemed to be a phase that passed when one reached full maturity. Overwhelmed and confused with these thoughts, Paul hurriedly left the China House to avoid Phoenix's seeing him. Never in his life had he been attracted to males. This turn of events had him baffled. He still enjoyed looking and becoming sexually aroused at certain female bodies, but this relationship with Phoenix was not a physical one. It was on a much deeper level. Paul was brought out of himself by hearing his name being called over and over. Rita, red-faced and out of breath, rushed over to throw her arms around his neck and kiss him. Her loose hair was being blown around. Wide eyed, flushed, and excited, she brought her body against his.

"Big man on the campus, I miss you. Why didn't you call me?" Rita rubbed herself against him and kissed his ear. "Lover, in my room are Johnny Six-Packs, all we need for a private party of our own."

Paul pulled away, saying, "Not now, Rita, I'm feeling antisocial and not in a party mood." Rejection flared into resentment, and Rita left hurriedly.

Later he could have kicked himself for refusing Rita. With her he could have behaved like a normal young man in bed, but he knew it to be just a short-term relationship. From what he had heard from the boys, Rita was a "butterfly woman."

After removal of her makeup and a change of clothes, Shau Feng went downstairs. She was elated because Aunt Sher Sher had praised her performance. Sher Sher told Shau Feng it was better that she and Charles leave as soon as possible, because even a blind man couldn't miss the marked resemblance between them, and it might become obvious that Phoenix looked too much like a female.

Stationed at the bottom of the stairs was a male reporter. When he saw Phoenix, he began shooting questions at her.

"Where did you learn Chinese Opera? Who was your teacher?" Sara came to Shau Feng's rescue, telling the man to speak slowly. She explained that Phoenix's comprehension of English was limited. When Rachel Lee observed the encounter with the reporter, she quickly brought a tray of soft drinks. She shoved a drink into the startled man's hand. Brenda followed on Rachel's heels with a tray of food. The girls blocked him, allowing Shau Feng to slip away from the reporter's questions.

Casi and Jim beckoned to Shau Feng. They congratulated their friend on the fine performance, and she in turn thanked them for their praise. Jim revealed *The Monkey King* story was unfamiliar to him.

Shau Feng replied, "Briefly, it's a folk epic about a roguish monkey that caused havoc in heaven. His penance was to accompany the monk Tripitaka to India for Buddhist Scriptures. The part that you just saw had to do with that ruined feast for the gods, in which the monkey ate all the peaches of immortality." Meanwhile, Casi's roving eyes ogled every woman he saw in the China House.

Jim directed Phoenix's attention to Casi. "Lost his latest girlfriend because of his wandering eyes. Can't you see the loss left him devastated, empty, a wreck, and brokenhearted, but our boy's a quick healer. He believes all Latin men are God's gift to women."

Casi, giving Phoenix a glowing smile, raised his right hand and said, "Honest to God, it's true. I swear it on my mother's head. I can smell a woman and locate her in the dark. We are born with the talent. It's in our genes. Cast your eyes at Sara Sing by the big window. She is secretly in love with me. Would you believe it? The other day, she begged me for a date!"

"Enough, Amigo Mio, your mind is creating your wildest subconscious desire. Sara Sing has a date list a mile long, with your name nowhere in sight. Phoenix, this Latin lad dreams up his own fantasies and tries to live them." Casi waved his hand with a gesture of dismissal at Jim.

Shau Feng said, "Enough, you two lovers are mad." Scanning the room, she raised an arm to get Jo-An's attention. The small woman came carrying a tray of food.

"Jo-An, here are two growing young men in need of nourishment." Casi's face took on a strange expression as he watched Phoenix departing.

Jim poked him in the ribs. "Grease face, why eyeball Phoenix?"

"Buddy, there is something strange about him. During my last visit home to see my mother—she has ESP—I asked her to pay particular attention to a picture of Phoenix in the newspaper. Mom peered at the picture and threw it back at me, accusing me in Spanish of being a half-wit for playing games with her."

Jim sagaciously nodded his head. "Your mother wasn't far from being wrong. Every parent knows his own child." Jim called out to Jo-An, "Little Darling, here we are."

She smiled at the both. "Good afternoon, Casi, Jim." The young men peered at the unfamiliar food on the tray. Jo-An said, "This red sauce is very hot; that yellow one is sweet." They selected a soft roll containing meat and dipped it into the hot sauce. Jim held the tray, with his fingers acting like a clamp. Jo-An couldn't take it away.

Casi said, "That was tasty. What do you call it?"

She said, "Bau. It's pronounced like the English word 'bow.' It's dough wrapped around meat, fish, or vegetables. They come steamed, baked, or fried."

Jim, pointing to another roll, said, "What is inside this roll?"

Jo-An studied the roll and said, "Oh, that—it's yesterday's roadkill."

Casi took a bite out of the bau. He said, "Jim, this one is also good. Let's try some more. Hey, you ape, don't leave your fingerprints on my food."

Jim, paying no attention to Casi, asked, "Jo-An, what's inside this one?"

She cocked her head to the side. "*Rechauffe.*"

"In English, My Sweet Child."

"Leftovers from last week's party."

Jim grinned. "I really adore this girl. Now, My Secret Love, why don't we relieve you of this heavy tray. It's much too heavy for a tot like you to carry." Jo-An set the tray on the nearest table. Casi eyed her body.

"Jo-An, when you grow up, I'll take you out on a date."

She stepped away. "What a revolting thought! Someday I shall grow up, but you never will." Away she went, toward the kitchen.

Jim said, "I told you Jo-An was smart." Along came Rachel, carrying a tray of drinks. "Gentlemen, care for something to wash down all that food?"

"Thank you, we would like to have some cherry soda."

"You're welcome." They watched Rachel move off to serve other people.

While they were eating, Jim said, "Casi, who in your opinion is more beautiful, Rachel or Sara?"

"They are equal, my friend."

"Have you ever asked Rachel for a date?"

"Yes, I have, and she then asked me for my zodiac sign. I'm a Taurus. Her face clouded as she told me that our signs weren't compatible, and so she wouldn't see me."

Jim replied, giving his friend a disappointing look, "You are incredibly stupid for a Latin. For a woman of that caliber, I would change my birthday."

9

Champs

The Plainfield Lions rode over the West Virginia Cougars 20 to 13. It was Plainfield College's first football championship in its entire existence. Pictures of the football players, coaches and Dr. Oriello covered the front pages of every magazine, newspaper, and sports gazette in the country. The news media praised Chet Harris's outstanding achievement, calling it a feather in his cap and a boost to his aged ego. The sportscasters had to agree that Chet hadn't lost his Midas touch. There were full-page photos of Phoenix jumping high into the air to catch the last touchdown of the game.

During the game, Shau Feng's eagerness to win had permeated the spirits of the Lions team. They fought hard against the prior year's division champs. With the score 14 to 13 in the Lions's favor, and a few seconds on the clock left to play, Paul was expected to eat the ball, ending the game. Instead he let loose with a Hail Mary pass in the direction where he thought Phoenix would be, across the goal line. The crowd came to their feet as Phoenix brought down the football. She landed just as the clock ran out of time. The cheering from the crowd was thunderous. Spectators scaled the short walls, running onto the playing field, swarming toward Shau Feng. She was almost cut off from her teammates. Shau Feng tossed the football into the crowd. They went for the ball as she scrambled for safety among her teammates.

Shau Feng was exhilarated from the excitement of winning. Robin, trotting along side her, said, "Little Shrimp, that catch will give the Eagles' scouts something to think about for the oncoming game. That fella you jumped against wasn't a johnny-come-lately peewee; he was last year's All-American." She was wildly greeted by the Lions players as they made their way to the locker room. Once inside, all hell broke loose. Chet and his assistant coaches were carried around the locker room on the players' shoulders. The noise level inside the crowded room was deafening. Chet lauded his assistant coaches and the team and tried to spirit Shau Feng out of the men's locker room to wait for the McGinnis people, the security men her aunt had hired to safeguard her. But Shau Feng and Chet couldn't get through the mob of reporters who were shoving their way through the door. Inside the locker room, they were being wedged in by the multitude of bodies. Reporters forced their way to Phoenix's side, shouting questions.

Mr. Harris put his strong arm around Phoenix and said, "Guys, please, give him a chance to catch his breath, and he will speak to you."

Phoenix paused before she spoke. "The credit doesn't belong to me; it also belongs to Mr. Harris, Mr. Claymore, Mr. Brown and the team. It was the coaches' game plan that lead us to win this division championship. It's a great honor for me to be on this team." A reporter shouted a question in her face. Suddenly a team of McGinnis men arrived. They whisked Shau Feng out of the locker room and away, amid the shouts of reporters.

Back in the hotel, Shau Feng soaked in a hot tub, soothing her muscles, which were aching from the pounding she had taken. Peering into the mirror, she remarked, "Shit, just look at the black-and-blue marks. I wonder what the others look like, after that battle royal. There was at least one consolation: We won." Shau Feng applied Chinese bruise medicine to the aching areas. She had decided that the national championship game would be the end of her football career. Sher Sher had extracted a promise from her, that she would stop acting like a tomboy. Shau Feng eyed her breasts, which were full like her aunt's, and thanked heaven she still was a female. Football was exciting, but it wasn't her bag. For Shau Feng, it would never replace the thrill she got from running.

Shau Feng was expected for dinner in the Lemar suite, so she hurriedly finished dressing and stopped her reverie. She decided on a bright-colored dress that Sher Sher would like. Shau Feng peered at her reflection in the mirror, pleased with what she saw. "Wouldn't everyone be surprised to see Phoenix Chen in a dress," she thought to herself.

The Plainfield Gladiators were making merry on the Sunday-evening bus back to their college. Music supplied by tape decks bounced off the walls of the bus. A proper party was planned upon their return to college. John read aloud from the Sunday paper about their exploits against the Cougars. Shau Feng sat in the rear seat alone, spreading herself on the seats. Fatigue took hold of the youths as the excitement died down. Each felt his own aches and pains. Chet, reclining in his seat, had the national championship game on his mind. This game would take place in New York City, two weeks from today. From viewing the tapes of the Academy Eagles numerous times, he realized they were the stronger team. His bright spots were Phoenix and Paul. He wondered, could we get away with Phoenix's masquerade until the final game?

Chet, Joe and Wilton mingled with the youths as they put on their protective equipment. The locker room was charged with anticipation. Many were chewing gum as a means of releasing their tension. Phoenix, who never dressed or undressed with the team, hadn't yet arrived. Thoughts of an accident crossed Pop's mind, but he immediately dismissed them. Chet reemphasized to the young men looking at him for guidance that this game was for all the marbles. Chet radiated confidence. He was glad to see his wife walk in with Phoenix completely dressed to play, carrying her helmet. She was lighthearted and gay. Her hair was stuffed under the fisherman's cap. The young woman greeted everyone as she made her way to Chet. Shau Feng paused to speak of victory to each player. Chet summoned Paul and drew him aside. "This Eagles team had held all their opponents this year to less than seventy yards. Mr. Armstrong, be alert; think on your feet. You can beat them."

"Yes, sir."

Shau Feng desired a word with Paul alone. She hung back in the locker room until almost everyone had left. Coming behind him quietly, she said, "Paul, this is my last game with the team." Recognition of Shau Feng's voice, caused Paul to tense up. An uncontrollable urge to kiss Phoenix came over him and made him furious with himself. In a fit of blind rage, he spun around to hit the locker door. His fist made contact with Phoenix's left eye. He realized what he had done and froze in shock. Instinctively, Shau Feng hit Paul in the stomach. He folded over. Her Chen palm zeroed in on the top of his forehead. Inches before it made contact, she stopped her hand. Her temper exploded, "Paul, you wang da ban [bastard], snake-in-the-grass! I hate you, you son-of-a-bitch!" She shoved him away from her. "This Chinese never wants to see your ugly American face again. Drop dead!" Mr. Brown came to the locker room for his two-way radio and heard the commotion. He went to investigate. One look at Phoenix's eye caused him to grab Paul by the jersey and push him out the door.

"Mr. Armstrong, get on the field now!" Returning to Phoenix, he said very softly, "Son, let me look at that eye." She showed it to him. "How did it happen?"

"It was my own fault. I wasn't looking where I was going."

"Don't bullshit me, Boy."

Charles was outside the Lions locker room, waiting for his niece to appear. He was there to wish her luck. Meanwhile, the big man was reminiscing about the good old days with a football buddy working at the stadium. When Shau Feng failed to come out and a young blond football player was shoved out the door, Charles excused himself and entered. Hearing Shau Feng's voice, he hurried toward it. Upon seeing a person holding something over Shau Feng's face, he sprang into action, grabbing the man under his armpits and lifting him off his feet.

"What are you doing to Phoenix? How would you like me to break your back?" Alarmed, Shau Feng spoke in Chinese.

"Uncle, please let him down. Mr. Brown is trying to help me. I must play in today's game." She removed an ice compress, exposing her eye to him.

Charles saw that the eye was almost closed. He coldly responded. "What are you—crazy? It's out of the question. . . . " Charles's head was moving side to side.

"Uncle, must I get on my knees to beg you?" Charles clamped his mouth shut. He thought for a moment. Mr. Brown was still shaken. Charles removed his sunglasses from his coat pocket. He fit them to Shau Feng's face. Without looking at Mr. Brown, he ordered adhesive tape. Shau Feng could hear her uncle swearing under his breath as he worked. Charles held her by the arms and looked at her face.

"Phoenix, you are dead meat if the Eagles discover you have a blind side. They are playing this game to win. Be extra careful, and never let your guard down on the field for a minute."

"Uncle, swear to me you will not tell Auntie. I beseech you. They need me."

"If Sher Sher finds out about the eye, she will leap on the field and drag you off."

"I shall be careful. Thank you for your help." Charles opened his coat and shirt to remove a gold chain from around his neck and gave it to his niece.

"This is your grandfather's lucky charm. I hope it gives you the same luck it gave him." She kissed his hands, then placed the chain over her head and tucked it under her jersey. She ran out of the room, placing the helmet over her head. Mr. Brown didn't understand what was being said in Chinese between them. Charles felt a knot forming in the pit of his stomach and wondered if he had done the right thing. If something happened to Shau Feng, would Sher Sher ever forgive him? Even worse, would he forgive himself?

"Mr. Lemar, don't worry. Phoenix can take care of himself." The big man slowly let the air out of his lungs.

"God, how I wish this game was over right now." The veins in his neck were bulging. Charles sat down to relax. He couldn't go to Sher Sher in this condition or all hell would break loose.

Phoenix was the last player of the Lions introduced to the crowd. They roared at the mention of the name. The Eagles' coaching staff looked upon Paul and Phoenix as their biggest threat. The Chinese kid was too fast for them to contain. Paul could dot an i with his passing. On the field, the Eagles won the toss. They elected to receive. From the moment the ball was in play, the Eagles went about their game plan. This mighty physical team was going to wear down their opponents. Paul was shaken by what he had done to Phoenix and the kid's hot words burned him. He was always under heavy pressure from the Eagles, resulting in his overthrowing his receivers. He purposely kept the ball away from Phoenix, so as not to put him in danger. That eye had looked bad to him. It was a grueling, punishing game, where neither side gave an inch. Paul was sacked three times and constantly driven out of the pocket. The Eagles' quarterback didn't have an easy time of it either. He too threw away the ball under heavy pressure. At the end of the half, the score was tied 0 to 0. It was a very tired crew that made their way into the Lions' locker room. Chet was proud of the way his team was playing.

Paul came to apologize to Phoenix, who was still wearing her helmet. She shoved him away. Paul bit his lip and went to sit in a corner. Chet had to admit his boys were playing against a stronger team, yet they were holding their own. They were dog tired as the coach went into his pep talk. While he spoke, Pop began to worry.

The young men weren't looking him in the eye. He could sense defeat in the air. The old man cut his speech short to allow them to rest. Out came his pipe, which he smoked while pondering the situation.

Phoenix looked from Chet to her teammates' faces. Her Chen chin pulled in as her temper skyrocketed. Up she stepped on the bench, asking for all their attention. There was bitterness in her voice as she said sharply, "Mr. Cool, you sad ass, did some devil steal your nerve? If you are unwilling to play, give the ball to someone who will." Her eyes roamed the faces of the young men. "Do you sorry Sams need a Chinese hick to show you what it takes to win? Little boys, are you tired and ready to give up? So you came up against a brick wall and sat on your rear ends to cry for your mothers. In China, we knock down mountains that stand in our way! Gentlemen, Pop Harris has made us a promise, which he kept. I don't know about you, but I came to New York not to *play* a football game, but to *win* one. Before us lies the glory road. Too damn bad if the road isn't to your liking! There are no free rides in life. Does a Lions jacket only mean something to impress the girls? Do you need a piece of cloth to prove you are men or get women to notice you? All I know is there are National Championship rings at the end of the glory road. In this game, second best gets no prizes. I for one will not go back to Plainfield College without honor. The Eagles will have to beat me—I ask for no quarter. I'm going to travel the glory road with or without you. You needn't burn your boats. Remain here where it is safe and warm. I shall not let Pop down!" Off the bench she went and stormed out the locker room door, not looking back.

The entire Lions team was on the sidelines, sitting on their benches in the cold, waiting for the half-time entertainment to finish. Chet was heartened to see the look of determination on the boys' faces, but was undecided whether to bench Paul or not. His first half's effort was inept. Perhaps he needed more time. Pop had

Bobby Gold warming up. Paul was known for doing the unexpected on the first play of the game or the quarter. After the kickoff, the Lions' receiver asked for a fair catch. He was surrounded by Eagles in a sea of white. Paul came out of the huddle to call the signals. The ball was snapped, and the Eagles blitzed the Lions on their own ten-yard line. Harry was coming fast for a hand off and slipped. He recovered, but lost his forward momentum. Robin made his way into the Eagle backfield, cutting across all the way to Paul's left, and raised his hands. The charging Eagles had their hands raised, blocking Paul's view of the field. Sensing where Phoenix was in the backfield, he tossed the ball to his friend, without realizing what he was doing. Paul aided Harry in stopping the Eagle charge. Phoenix, with the ball, saw Robin was open and alone in the Eagle backfield. Jim and Casi opened a hole in the Eagle line. The Eagles' safeties rushed in, in an attempt to close the gap. Phoenix faked a run, drawing the Eagles toward the hole in their line. Then she stopped and backpedaled into the pocket behind Paul and Harry. Quickly the ball left her hands, heading in Robin's direction. Robin caught the ball and raced for the goal line. The Eagle safeties tried to catch him, but the young man had too much of a lead and proved too fleet-footed. Robin crossed the goal line and began to strut about, showing the ball to the spectators. He shouted, "Phoenix is going for all the marbles in this game."

The roar of the crowd died, and was followed by silence. Just as Charles had predicted, an Eagle nose tackle came along Phoenix's blind side to hit her, and Phoenix Chen lay on the ground not moving, with blood trickling out of the side of her mouth. She was carried off the field to the medical department. Paul peered at his fallen friend. He cursed himself for being a coward. It should have been him on the ground, not Phoenix. Bitterness set in, and Paul threw off all past restraint. He ordered the guys pushing the Eagles about the field, "Leave them alone! Let's show these suckers our stuff."

The assistant coach of the Eagle defensive squad encouraged

his players to demoralize the Lions. On the face-off for the extra point, the Eagle linemen boasted about how they had taken out Phoenix. Some joked about the blood coming from Phoenix's mouth. These gladiators declared, "More of the Lions are going to be carried off the field on stretchers before this game is over." Abu, the Lions' punter, kicked for the extra point and was on target. Upon returning to the sidelines, the Lions informed their fellow players about the threat they had received from the Eagles.

When Abu kicked the ball, the Eagle receiver caught the ball, tried to run, and was immediately smothered by Lions. He was hit very hard and needed to be escorted off the field. Now the Eagles found themselves being bombarded with Lions breaching their lines. Play after play, the Eagle quarterback was forced out of the pocket for a hurried pass. Led by Silent Sam, the Lions' linemen tore the jersey off the Eagles' quarterback's body. Sam seemed to be everywhere in the Eagles' backfield. The men assigned to guard him were thrown to the ground. All the Eagles' efforts never made the line of scrimmage. The rough-and-tumble fights at the scrimmage line increased. Tempers flared on both sides as they shoved each other. Johnny the Bear dropped the fullback in the next play for a big loss.

Watching his young men maul the Eagles, Chet couldn't believe his eyes. Joe and Wilton were elated as they patted their charges on the back, urging them on. The pride on the faces of the Lions was mixed with anger and determination. Chet's young men were playing like seasoned fighters on the battlefield.

The reporters who were broadcasting from the press box in the stadium said that Paul was executing the plays with skill. He brought the Lions team steadily down the field while eating up the clock as they overpowered the Eagles. Harry the Horse blasted his way through the Eagles' line to score their second touchdown of the game, which was a thirty-yard carry. When the Eagles received the ball, they couldn't get a play started to counter the Lions' scoring machine. Silent Sam and Johnny the Bear leaned heavily on the

Eagle backfield. This time, Paul brought his men to the Eagle one-yard line. The Eagles bunched up, and Bronco came to the line and vaulted over for a touchdown.

The fourth quarter became worse for the Eagles. Their coaches tried to tighten up their defense and get the ball moving, but they couldn't stop the Lions. Even the clock was against them. It had two minutes of playing time left.

Chet sent his wife to the medical center to find out about Phoenix so she could report back on her condition. Chet was astonished at the players for the effort they put into this game. They were beating the Eagles at their own game plan. Chet called time out, and Paul came to the sidelines to talk to the Coach. He reminded Paul that there was a minute left on the clock to end the game. They had the ball and four downs to go. Chet cautioned Paul against losing the ball. He went back into the huddle. There was a long call. The ball was snapped. Paul threw a pass to Stretch, who made a Phoenixlike one-handed catch, running down the sideline and across the goal line. After the kick for the extra point, the game was over. Chet trotted to shake Wild Bill's hand, and Bill asked about Phoenix. Chet smiled, telling him the kid was fine. Bill praised what Chet had done with the Lions. Meanwhile the Lions players went to their locker on rubbery legs. They were bone-tired, but their exhaustion was overridden by anger, was caused by the fact that the Eagles' cheap shot had put their friend Phoenix out of the game. Once inside the locker room, they allowed themselves to collapse.

After Phoenix had been carried to the medical center, Charles was on his feet, dragging Sher Sher, who had clamped a hold on the back of his jacket. For a big man, Charles moved very fast. The McGinnis men were behind them, following the Titan on the run. Sher Sher barked orders at the one with a cellular phone. Charles hurried in the direction of the medical room.

They arrived at the medical center at the same time as the stretcher-bearers carrying Shau Feng. A guard attempted to block

Charles from entering the room, but he effortlessly forced himself past. Another security guard stepped in front of him, only to be brushed aside. Once the Lemars were inside the medical center, Sher Sher elbowed her way to the doctor's side. He was in the process of removing Phoenix's helmet. She whispered in the doctor's ear, "Don't undress Phoenix—Phoenix is a girl."

Dr. Rangi, a tall, thin, delicate-looking Indian, turned to face Sher Sher. His eyes went from his patient to Sher Sher. He straightened up and shouted, "Security, clear the room at once. Let only the family members remain." Charles and the McGinnis men helped the guards clear the room. He stationed himself in front of the door, allowing the guards to close it.

The TV monitor was showing the championship game in the medical center. After the helmet had been removed from Phoenix's head, the doctor saw the taped-on sunglasses. He took them off and saw that the patient's left eye was swollen closed and discolored. Before ordering X rays, Dr. Rangi carefully examined the closed eye. Sher Sher recognized the sunglasses and placed them in her purse. On further examination, the doctor observed Phoenix's split lip and a cut inside her mouth.

The X rays revealed no damage to the head. Dr. Rangi suggested that Sher Sher take Phoenix to another doctor for a second opinion and have an ophthalmologist examine her eye. Sher Sher nodded, asking about the blood coming from the mouth. She was told that it was from a minor cut on the inside of her mouth and a split lip. Meanwhile, Shau Feng showed signs of recovering. She opened her eyes, peering around the room and attempted to get to her feet and saying, "I must return to the game!" Too weak to stand, she fell back, and Sher Sher restrained her from getting up.

"Shau Feng, your teammates are playing the game of their lives." Shau Feng realized that Sher Sher had seen her closed black eye and would never allow her to reenter the game.

Ms. Teresa Granger, a reporter, left the crowd around the medical room for a smoke. As she worked her way through to a vacant area near the gate of the medical center, her attention was drawn to a young Chinese woman crying. She wondered if the young woman knew Phoenix Chen. Teresa had learned to speak and write Chinese, when she had been stationed in Taiwan as a TV correspondent. Teresa threw away her cigarette and approached Diana Wu. Teresa sympathetically soothed Diana in Chinese. Hearing a friendly voice, Diana sobbed out the entire story, about Shau Feng and the Lions. Teresa couldn't believe her ears. Could it be possible that Shau Feng and Phoenix were the same person? "Little Phoenix" was a girl's name in Chinese.

Charles, who was outside the medical room, came in and informed Sher Sher that Diana Wu was speaking to a reporter. Teresa saw a frightened look come over Diana's face. She was staring directly over her head. Teresa turned to face a stern Sher Sher, whose eyes were filled with fire. Theresa asked about Shau Feng's condition in Chinese. Sher Sher brushed the reporter aside, grabbed Diana by the cowl of her coat, and shoved her inside the medical center.

Sher Sher walked back to face Teresa. The reporter held out a hand, displaying a professional smile, and said, "Granger of TV."

Sher Sher took her hand in a viselike grip, causing Teresa to wince, and she said, in Chinese, "If you dare write anything unfavorable about my niece, I'll personally knock your head off." Sparks flew between the women. Neither side blinked as they locked eyes.

Teresa's fingers were numb. She said, "Who the hell do you think you are, Lady?"

Sher Sher asserted, "I shall do whatever must be done to protect Shau Feng. Don't misunderstand me! Hurt Shau Feng in your story, and you'll regret it." Ms. Granger watched as the Chinese woman hurried away, back to the medical center.

Fred Roper, another reporter, came over to Teresa and asked, "What's up, Teresa? Do you know the tigress of Cincinnati?"

Teresa forced a weak smile while fumbling about in her purse for a cigarette. "That woman can be ruthless when she's crossed, with a track record to prove it." The food in Teresa's stomach turned sour. She opened her purse, searching for an antacid pill. Masking her failing nerves, her hands shaking, slowly she walked to the water fountain. Teresa pulled herself together, armed with the sense of righteousness that a reporter has on the verge of a coup. She mentally prepared herself for battle. Giving the appearance of being calm, Teresa returned to the other reporters, who were awaiting news about Phoenix Chen's condition.

Shau Feng was on her feet as Diana came through the door. Upon seeing Shau Feng, she turned ashen, her body trembled violently, and tears flowed down her cheeks. She was crushed. She had betrayed Shau Feng's trust. Tears alone couldn't wash away her feeling of guilt.

Shau Feng said to her friend, "Diana, I'm okay. Don't cry."

Minutes later, in came Sher Sher, glaring at Diana. She advanced toward Diana and said, in Chinese, "Just look at yourself, sobbing like a baby. Stop it this very minute! If you don't, I'll give you something to cry about. How could you reveal Shau Feng's secret to a reporter? Where was your head?" Diana cowered against a wall. She sank to her knees.

Sher Sher coldly said, "Miss Diana Wu, what will you do to undo the damage you have done to Shau Feng?" Diana bowed her head and said, "Anything."

Shau Feng's heart was pounding. She wanted to ask Diana questions, but held her tongue until they were alone.

Sher Sher needed to be reassured that her niece hadn't sustained any permanent injury. She formulated a plan for Shau Feng's departure. She asked Dr. Rangi to arrange a spare nurse's uniform. Afterward, the doctor carried out Sher Sher's orders. Diana and

Shau Feng went behind a screen to change clothes.

Shau Feng grabbed her friend Diana's arms, shaking her vigorously. In a low voice, she said, "Diana, tell me what happened." Diana, not looking at Shau Feng, told her of the encounter with the woman reporter outside the medical room. Shau Feng caressed Diana's cheek with a hand. "The truth was bound to come out sooner or later. It's no big deal.... Auntie has a plan for us to leave here undetected. I would like you to act on my behalf when you return to the China House, while I am somewhere else."

Diana's confidence returned. She reassured herself, "I shall not fail Shau Feng again."

Sher Sher checked Diana's appearance in a nurse's uniform. She applied makeup to Diana's face and rearranged her hair to change her appearance, to make her look older. Meanwhile, on the TV monitor, the football game was still being played.

Charles entered the room and informed his wife that the McGinnis men were in position for the great exit. Shau Feng told Sher Sher in Chinese that Diana would be in her room at the China House to receive and transfer any messages to her while she was away from the public eye. Sher Sher protested. Shau Feng took a firm stand against her aunt on this point. Sher Sher realized that this wasn't the time or place to fight with Shau Feng. She agreed. Shau Feng asked Diana to sleep in her room and to let nobody in. She would call her every night at 9:00 P.M. Sher Sher covered Shau Feng's head and face with a scarf; then she came over and to Diana and whispered, "After you leave here, don't return to your hotel room, but go back directly to Plainfield College."

"I understand," said Diana.

Dr. Rangi made a call to the head nurse at St. Martin's Hospital, in Manhattan, to ask her for a favor. She was to tell all inquirers who come to the hospital asking about Phoenix Chen that the youth was sleeping. Then Dr. Rangi went outside to make an announcement, concerning Phoenix Chen's condition, to the reporters.

Dr. Rangi said, "Let me have your attention, or I'll go back into the room, telling you nothing." The reporters stopped shouting. He continued, "After examining Phoenix Chen, I found a split lower lip, a small cut inside the mouth, and a sign of a mild concussion. There was nothing on the X rays to cause any alarm." He didn't mention about Shau Feng's closed eye. Shau Feng had asked him not to say anything about it. "Phoenix Chen is being sent to St. Martin's hospital for overnight observation. Any questions?"

While the doctor had the crowd's attention, Diana left as a nurse. Sher Sher and Charles exited with Shau Feng, who was now in Diana's clothes and could be mistaken for Diana. Once out of the reporters' sight, the McGinnis men came to escort the Lemars and Diana on their separate ways.

In the McGinnis agents' car, Diana requested the McGinnis operator to drive her to the airport, but the man said he had instructions to drive her directly to Plainfield College.

During the ride out of the city, Diana glanced at her watch. The football game would have been over an hour ago, and her girlfriends would be back in their hotel rooms. She was supposed to report to them about Shau Feng's condition. Diana asked the agent if she could use his phone. She dialed the hotel phone number and gave the operator Amanda's room number. Upon hearing Amanda's voice, she said, in Chinese, "This is Diana. The masquerade is over. Tell everyone to keep their silence."

"Right, we will do it." The word spread among the Chinese like wildfire. Up went a yellow wall of silence about Shau Feng's identity.

Right after the game, inside the Lions' locker room, there was a scene of pandemonium. Photographers, sportsmen, Plainfield alumni, celebrities, and well-wishers pushed each other to congratulate the coaches and players. Chet acted like the pro he was and thanked them for their praise. Some of them asked Mrs. Harris repeatedly about Phoenix. She repeated what the doctor had announced to the reporters. Paul was besieged by reporters, but he pushed them aside, walking away.

Chet called over Paul, who shook his hand and said, "Mr. Harris, sir, thank you for the opportunity of a lifetime. You are the greatest coach in the world." A reporter asked Paul about the first touchdown play. Paul credited it to Chet and praised the Eagles and their fine coaching staff for the excellent game they had coached. He avowed that the Eagles had lost because Phoenix had helped to fire the team into a strong unit. In his mind, he said, "Phoenix, you surely earned your championship ring. We won by emulating your effort and fighting spirit. In the same spirit you possess, I learned to be honest and truthful by explaining my real feelings. The ghosts of the past that haunted me are gradually disappearing and lessening their power over me. Mr. Phoenix, one way or the other, I intend to maintain our friendship."

In the China House reception room, Bruce was among the Chinese students who remained at the college, gluing themselves to the screen while watching the championship game being played in New York City. During the first half of the game, Bruce suspected something was amiss. It was clear that Paul was keeping the ball away from Shau Feng. There were a few times when she was free of her coverage, but the throw went to Stretch. Bruce was only interested in how Shau Feng fared. Shau Feng had announced before leaving for New York that this would be her final game as a Lions player. Bruce concluded that the feminists would idolize Shau Feng whether the team won or lost.

On the first play of the third quarter, Paul's unexpected lateral to Shau Feng brought Bruce to the edge of his chair. The play caused the rushing Eagle line to pause as they changed direction.

There on the screen was Robin, alone in the Eagles' backfield. The next picture showed that Shau Feng was throwing the football from behind Paul and Harry. Now the action went to Robin and his touchdown run. He strutted with the ball in his hand. When the camera went to Phoenix lying on the ground, a replay showed Phoenix being hit by an Eagle after the ball was in Robin's hands. To Bruce's way of thinking, Shau Feng was employing her theatrical talent to dramatically end her football career with the Lions. He was certain with her Chi Gung, her internal strength, she couldn't be hurt. When the play resumed, he saw the Lions going after the Eagles' scalp.

A face-to-face encounter with Mrs. Sher Sher Lemar led Teresa to believe that the woman was a force to be reckoned with. Mrs. Sher Sher Lemar was very wealthy, fiercely family-loyal, and was certain to act to protect Shau Feng in a sensational story. Teresa must be very careful as to how the story was presented to the public. Teresa thought, "Shau Feng Chen has become headlines. If I don't write the story, somebody else will. First I must gather all the facts before presenting them to the public." She went to her terminal, accessing the computer library, and started to browse the screen. While reading the sports stories and listening to the audio, she said, "Diana said that Shau Feng did it for the honor of the Chinese and for the sake of Chet Harris." While browsing the screen, she froze the shot of Shau Feng, then placed it side by side for comparison with a picture of Mrs. Sher Sher Lemar. There was no doubt about the marked resemblance between those two women. She continued to view the film clips of Shau Feng interviews. Teresa commented, "Why did she downplay her ability?" Continuing to watch the screen, she smoked a cigarette. "I like this young woman. She had nerve and class. How did she avoid dressing and undressing in the men's locker room? I'll be damned—I'll bet Chet was in on it!" A picture of Shau Feng with Chet Harris came on the screen. "Son of a gun! How devilish can you be? The machos will cry in their beer—a girl playing football on a championship football team! Down will fall the bastions of manhood that exclude women from a purely masculine sport. Lord, what a hue and cry there will be." The reporter's fingers still ached from shaking hands with Sher Sher.

She reached into a bottom drawer and removed a bottle of whiskey. With a cigarette dangling from the side of her mouth, Teresa typed with two fingers. She laughed at herself when she realized she had assumed the posture of an old-time male reporter. The sports world would be in for a shock upon learning of the great deception. Shau Feng Chen, posing as Phoenix, a male student, was playing with the Plainfield Lions. It was a cooperative cover-up by the coach and the Chinese students at Plainfield College. The headlines would read, "Chet Harris beat the Eagles with a young Chinese woman on his team." The body of the story would emphasize the details of Shau Feng's disguise. Teresa searched her purse for another cigarette and continued, "Diana said that Shau Feng always arrived at each game in uniform and was spirited away after the game by the McGinnis Agency men and her supporters." Teresa had some thoughts. "How did she get away with it? Was she that good an actress to fool everyone? I don't believe that this couldn't happen without a mass participation—but then, people tend to believe almost anything when their suspicions are not aroused.

It was 6:00 A.M. Jim rapped on Paul's hotel door. There was a newspaper tucked under his arm. When there was no response, the African-American turned the doorknob. With a push, it swung away on its hinges. There he saw Paul, fully dressed on his bed. Jim turned on the lights and closed the door behind him. Paul, with his eyes open, was staring at the ceiling, ignoring Jim's presence. Jim displayed the newspaper headlines to Paul. He said, "Hey, Lost Soul, have you read today's news? A reporter, Ms. Teresa Granger, alleges that Phoenix Chen is a *girl*—named Chen Shau Feng. You know Phoenix better than anyone—what do you think?" Paul uprighted himself without looking at the newspaper. In a weak voice, he replied, "The story is true. I can hardly believe such great news. Chen Shau Feng is a woman." He repeated it aloud several times. "God, was I blind and deaf! When I first met her, she told me that she wasn't a boy, and my instincts told me she was feminine!" Paul's fingers were toying with the jade Buddha around his neck that Shau Feng had given him, while Jim was grinning from ear to ear, hearing Paul correctly pronounce Phoenix's Chinese name, Chen Shau Feng.

In her hotel room, when Dr. Oriello read the headlines of the newspaper, she immediately called her secretary at Plainfield College and asked, "Toby, check the personal records on Phoenix Chen. Call me back as soon as possible. Dear God, I remember Mrs. Sher Sher Lemar saying her *niece* was coming to Plainfield. I understand that Chinese pronounced the same sound for both 'he' and 'she,' but it is written differently". Minutes before, Gabriella had phoned St. Martin's Hospital to check on Phoenix Chen's condition. When the head nurse had informed her that there was no such person admitted to the hospital, she had called Chet immediately and blurted out, "Tell me whether the news story is true or not: Is Phoenix a female?" Chet answered promptly and tried to calm Dr. Oriello.

"Yes," he said. "The story is true. Both Lois and I were privy to it from the beginning. I apologize for the discomfort you must feel at being left out of this. But you should feel very proud that one of your female students achieved such success and paved the way for young women just entering the institution." He had barely finished when Gabriella hung up, eager to start taking compliments from the public.

Chet turned to Lois, who had her arms outstretched to him.

"What do you think, my dear? Shall we stay, or shall I retire? If I stay, there will be a huge uproar, and I'll have to face a lot of criticism."

Lois answered, "When have you ever run away from a fight? Let's stay, clear the air, and then we can leave with a clear conscience. Now, let's call Mrs. Sher Sher Lemar and ask her about Shau Feng."

Jim sat on a chair and dropped the newspaper to the floor. "Paul, old friend," he said, "talk to me." He arose from the bed to pace back and forth.

"Well," said Paul, "Around 11:00 P.M. last night, I left the celebration dinner to visit the hospital. The nurse on duty informed me that Phoenix Chen wasn't receiving any visitors until tomorrow. I took a cab to Chinatown, looking for a shrine. Phoenix is a Buddhist. I wanted to light joss sticks and pray for him as they do in China. I located a temple. Inside, I saw a monk behind a desk piled high with books. He was explaining the writings on a red piece of paper for an elderly Chinese man. After I lit three joss sticks for our friend, I sat on a bench. Suddenly, the old man turned his head and shouted at the children. 'Shau Feng, stop making a racket.' I looked at the little boy pointing to the little girl. I asked the old man if Shau Feng meant Phoenix in Chinese. He looked at me and said, 'Yes, Shau Feng in English means "Little Phoenix." It's a girl's name. Boys are called dragons.' It seemed like proof-positive from heaven, the purpose of which was to arouse this sleepwalker. Jim, I have been in love with Phoenix for many months. It tore me apart to think Phoenix was a boy. Every time I looked at Phoenix, I felt a female presence. In the locker room on the day of the National Championship, after everyone left, Phoenix came over to talk to me. I had been avoiding her for weeks. Upon recognizing her voice, I had the urge to kiss her. I lost control of myself. I swung about to hit a locker, but, unfortunately, she was in the way of my fist. I hit her in the eye. Jim, she played the entire first half of the game with one eye closed! I purposely kept the ball away from her. The opening play of the third quarter, as I was being blitzed, my toss to her was a reflex, not something planned. I alone am to blame for her getting hurt. After she was carried off the field, I pushed myself to excel and win for Phoenix."

Jim peered at Paul. He thought it humorous that Paul now referred to Phoenix as "she." In all the months he had known Paul, this was the most he had ever gotten out of him.

"Paul," he declared, "you are a klutz, born with nothing but mazel. Have you bothered to watch the reruns of the game on TV?" Paul shook his head. He ceased pacing the floor. "I thought so. All the sportscasters are lauding your textbook performance. Your so-called keeping the ball away from Phoenix was called 'playing lame duck.' Phoenix had driven the Eagle backfield wild during the first half of the game. Robin went unnoticed in their backfield during that third-quarter opening play, because the Eagles expected Phoenix, not Harry, to run the ball. Casi and Jim had made a hole in their line. Phoenix could have flown through that space with ease. That pass Phoenix threw to Robin caught the Eagles off guard. You idiot, on film, you were recorded throwing blocks, which knocked the Eagle linemen on their asses. Quarterbacks aren't supposed to block. There isn't one football coach in the country who hasn't added that play to his book. Now, to relieve your guilt trip, Phoenix was hit after Robin was on his way to the goal. The Eagles were gunning for Phoenix and you. With Phoenix being revealed as a girl, Coach Harris will become a living legend. As for that eye thing, Dr. Rangi stated publicly, 'No eye injury.'" Jim got to his feet and grabbed Paul and shook him violently. "Redneck moron, listen to me, and use your head. Keep your mouth shut about Phoenix until it becomes public knowledge."

It was 10:00 A.M. Dressed in a dark-blue suit and a white blouse, wearing black-rimmed glasses, Dr. Oriello stood on the dais of the hotel conference room. Her professional smile masked the tension she felt. Chet was seated next to Lois in the rear. Dr. Oriello beckoned to Chet to come up on the podium. Lois whispered to him, "Chet, you'd better go. Gabby needs you there." He slowly rose, with head held high, and walked straight down the aisle. To his amazement, the reporters rose and applauded. Chet looked at their faces and was overwhelmed by the admiration he saw. He stood on the podium, waved, and sat.

Dr. Oriello raised her arms for silence and asked the audience to be seated. It took a few minutes before they settled down. Dr. Oriello spoke into the microphone, in a clear voice, "Ladies and gentlemen, may I have your attention please. I have a note to read from Phoenix Chen." Gabriella read:

I, Chen Shau Feng, the Little Phoenix, am a female. The choice to play football for the Plainfield Lions as a boy was my own. Nobody coerced me into making the decision. My support came from my aunt and uncle, Mr. and Mrs. Harris, and my grandfather. Although they worried about me, they were my most staunch helpers. The doctors who examined me stated I was slightly injured. There was a minor cut inside my mouth that caused all the blood—a split lip, which is now swollen. It looked worse than it was. When the doctors learned the reason I gave for playing football, they concluded that I should have my head examined. Well, these learned gentlemen are entitled to their opinion, and I mine. It was a great honor and privilege for me to be able to play under the great coach Chet Harris. This talented man assembled a team that we at Plainfield College can look back upon with pride. My teammates will always have a special place in my heart. I commend every one of them on our victory. They all ought to be proud of the effort they made on the field yesterday in New York City. I harbor no hard feelings against the Eagles player who took me out of the game. I would have tried to do it to him, had I been in his place. Mr. Harris, what more can I say, except thanks for sharing your vast knowledge with me. Under your leadership and with the help of Mr. Brown and Mr. Claymore, we won a national championship. You and I have demonstrated that a woman can play football as well as a man.

I shall be out of the public eye for the time being. Should I choose to return to play football, I shall not go about dressing as a boy, but as a young woman. May God bless you and keep you. I remain, always, Chen Shau Feng, the Little Phoenix.

Chet rose to his feet and led the loud applause with his words coming slow and deliberately. "Chen Shau Feng," he said, "demonstrated that women can play football. I have also demonstrated that an old person or a retired one isn't ready to be put out to pasture. It took great courage for Shau Feng to enter a man's sport and show she could perform as a football player. Her actions have paved the way for women to attempt the same thing. May the future bring us more women like Chen Shau Feng." As he sat down next to his wife, the applause was deafening, and there were tears in her eyes when all the women rose, giving Chet Harris a standing ovation as a sign of respect.

10

The Finale

Wednesday night, Diana was alone in Shau Feng's room, eating her supper. The young Chinese woman had dug her nails into her palms, to still her tongue from talking too much. Diana, heartbroken over a slip of her tongue, was determined not to betray Shau Feng a second time. Suffering from a sense of guilt, she spoke to the four walls as if conversing with Shau Feng. In all Diana's life, her mother had overly protected her, and Diana had grown up timid and afraid to try things. From her mother's standpoint, men were evil and only interested in sex. Shau Feng had given her encouragement and showed her what a woman could accomplish. This interregnum was what she had needed to change her attitudes.

Reporters and visitors came to the campus seeking information about Shau Feng and her background. Knowing that Diana was Shau Feng's friend, they sought her out. Diana stood her ground, withstanding their insistence and angry words. She only told the reporters that Shau Feng was at home, resting. Some Chinese young men accompanied Diana to her classes, acting as buffers. Amanda, annoyed at some of the aggressive reporters, struck the abusive jerks in the shin with a small club. Nobody was allowed to bully Diana. May Lee lost her temper more than once and ripped cameras out of reporters' hands for being overly aggressive toward Diana.

Diana, in Shau Feng's room, was reading a book when the phone rang, startling her. She answered the phone and recognized the voice immediately.

"How are you, Diana?"

"I'm well, thank you."

"I missed you so much these last few days. It's all over. Now you can tell everyone that my grandfather died on the morning of the national championship game. The old master was put to rest beside Lavender. Dr. Oriello was under the impression that I was somewhere in the United States, but I'm actually in Hong Kong. Let her hear the news from TV. This Saturday, we shall be in Middletown, Ohio, around noon. Will you please come for the weekend?"

Diana's spirit soared as she firmly answered, "Shau Feng, I shall be at the Lemar Estate awaiting your arrival."

"From now on, Diana, I shall treat you like a sister. I am truly sorry for the suffering I caused you. Can you ever forgive me?"

Diana, overcome with emotion, cried, "There is nothing to forgive."

"Good night, Diana."

"Good night, Shau Feng."

Diana emerged from Shau Feng's room and saw Tom Lee coming up the stairs. She requested that he help her assemble the students in the reception room. In less than ten minutes, all the students in the China House were downstairs waiting for Diana. Diana walked downstairs and stopped on the third step from the bottom. She peered into the faces and began. "Shau Feng is on the way back from Hong Kong, where she was attending her grandpa Lee Chen's funeral. This weekend I will be at the Lemar Estate. Brothers and sisters of China, I thank you for your full support on behalf of Shau Feng. I appreciate the cooperation you all gave me. Bless you all." Diana bowed deeply.

Bruce quickly shattered the silence that followed by applauding. He shouted, "Well done, Miss Wu." Diana, who had tasted the bitterness of despair, now was bathed in admiration. She turned to hide her tears. Like steel filings attracted by a magnetic force, her friends came to comfort her. Bruce spoke.

"Diana Wu, now I understand why Shau Feng had chosen you to handle her affairs on her behalf. Both of you are alike in strength." Diana thanked Bruce for his kind words. She felt a weight had been lifted from her shoulders. Slowly she left the crowd and climbed the stairs. It was the combined forces of Sher Sher's anger and Shau Feng's love that transformed Diana from a frightened girl into a strong woman.

Bruce's eyes never left Diana. For the first time in his life, he saw a woman whom he wanted to marry. He wondered about all that had transpired, whether she felt the same way about him. He would have to plan a way to court her and win her.

Jo-An volunteered to go to the Frank Caruso House and Susan B. Anthony House that very evening, to make the announcement about Shau Feng's return. The young women knew a telephone call would do, but they urged Jo-An to go and hurried upstairs to help Jo-An select an outfit. They settled on a royal-blue dress, a tank-top blouse, and fake-fur–trimmed boots. The young women inspected Jo-An and voiced their approval. Jo-An's face radiated happiness. Sara placed a camel-hair coat over Jo-An's shoulders. Rachel sprayed her with French perfume. They accompanied her to the door and watched her walk away.

Jo-An opened the door of the Caruso House. The warm air struck her flushed red cheeks. She walked over to the desk, pushing her coat hood back. The youth on duty, without looking up from his book, smelled the air, and glanced up at her.

"What can I do for you, doll?"

"I would like to address all the students in this house."

He raised his eyes to study her face. "What is your name and the nature of the announcement?"

"I am Jo-An Han, and it's about Phoenix Chen." Stu was out of the chair at the mention of Phoenix.

"Tim, get Bronco. Assemble the troops. Move, man, move!" Stu came around the desk to Jo-An.

"Miss Han, would you care to have a seat?"

"No, thank you, I'll stand." There was the sound of someone running down the stairs.

Harry came flying down, two steps at a time. He was wearing slacks and a T shirt. Harry's bulging arm muscles look as if they were carved of stone. He appeared to have been sleeping in his clothes. When he saw Jo-An, the muscles in his jaw twitched. Harry, facing Stu, grunted, "Did you leave your manners at home? Why didn't you offer the young lady a seat?" Jo-An touched Harry's wrist. He looked at her and smiled.

"It's all right. Stu offered me a chair, but I chose to stand."

"Good Evening, Miss Han."

"Good Evening, Harry."

"Can I get you some refreshments?"

"No, thank you. I came to make an announcement about Shau Feng." Bronco was now behind his cousin, moving around him. His hair was uncombed, his face needed a shave, and he was sloppily dressed.

"Good evening, Miss Han. I hope you are well?"

"I'm fine, thank you. I have come to make an announcement about Shau Feng."

"Allow me to escort you to our reception hall."

The curious students gathered in the room. Bronco lifted her on top of a table, where she looked down at the young men.

"Gentlemen, Mr. Lee Chen, Shau Feng's grandfather, died the morning of the national Championship Game, in Hong Kong. Her family flew to Hong Kong on that date, and Shau Feng joined them for the burial. In Lee's will, the retired actor requested a quiet burial away from the public eye, and his family complied with his last wish. Shau Feng will be present at the celebration next Saturday. For those who wish to send condolence cards, forward them to the China House. Thank you for your attention. Gentlemen, I bid you a good night."

While Jo-An was giving her speech, she noticed Bronco looking steadily at her. When she finished talking, he helped her off the table.

"Jo-An, where are you off to now?"

"I'm going to deliver the same message at the Anthony House."

"I'll accompany you."

"Don't bother, Bronco."

"It's no bother; it would be my pleasure."

Harry escorted Jo-An to a chair and excused himself. Her coat was hung on a coat tree. He reappeared, carrying a tray with a cup of hot chocolate and some cookies. The young man placed the tray on a table next to Jo-An. She thanked Harry.

Paul emerged from the crowd and greeted Jo-An. A quick glance displayed that Paul's appearance had improved. She smiled at him. Paul said, "Jo-An, you look very stunning tonight."

"Thank you, Paul."

"By any chance, have you Shau Feng's telephone number?"

"No, I don't, but you could ask Diana."

"I did, many times, without any results."

"Things have changed as of tonight. Why not ask her again? Are you afraid to enter the China House?"

"No, I'm not! Thank you, Jo-An. Good Night."

"Good Night, Paul." Jo-An drank some hot chocolate. A shout caused her to pause while drinking. "Paul, you crazy man, put on this coat. It's freezing outside."

Teresa had purchased a new outfit for tonight's nationwide TV broadcast. This Wednesday-night show was her big break. It all started when she was a young woman fresh out of college. She had enlisted in the foreign-affairs department to see the world. The government had sent her to Taiwan to do documentaries on local culture and heritage. While in Taiwan, she learned to read, write, and speak Chinese. When her enlistment was up, she returned to the States.

On her way out the apartment lobby, she was intercepted by two Chinese men. "Ms. Granger?"

"Yes?" Teresa replied timidly. Their sudden appearance out of nowhere upset her. Her hands were trembling, but she tried not to show it. The taller man pushed an envelope into her hand. Her heart was pounding. Looking at the envelope in her hand, Teresa tore it open. Inside was a section from a Chinese newspaper. There were a column of characters highlighted in yellow. Out came the glasses from her small purse. Laboriously she translated the Chinese characters into English, in her head.

"Lee Chen, the retired popular movie actor, beloved TV personality, and opera star, died in Hong Kong on this date, and it was his last wish to have a quiet funeral, out of the public eye in which he had spent all his life. We all mourn his passing and send condolences to his daughter and granddaughter."

Teresa asked herself, "So what?" Then she reread the item. All at once, it hit her. Chen—the date Mr. Chen died was the same as the date of the National Championship College Football game.... Out of the public eye... family... Teresa felt proud of herself. She had been right all along; Shau Feng wasn't hiding. And those Chen women were real women, for sure.

On a prime-time nationwide TV news broadcast, during the sports segment of the show, the anchorperson asked Ms. Granger the usual question: "Do you know where Miss Shau Feng Chen is?" Teresa looked directly into the camera and read from the paper:

"Miss Shau Feng Chen and family, please accept my condolences and those of the entire staff of WTV news, on the passing of your grandfather Lee Chen. The Chen family, in keeping with Lee's last wish, had a quiet burial out of the public eye. Those of you who wish to send condolence cards, address them to: Ms. Shau

Feng Chen, Miss Little Phoenix Chen, or Phoenix, in care of the China House, Plainfield College, Plainfield, Ohio. Thank you and good night." Before Teresa was out of the chair, the news show's phone switch boards had all lit up. Her boss came running over. Teresa prepared herself for his anger. But he threw his arms around her, lifting her off the floor.

"Teresa, Baby, Darling, I love you!"

The raging fires inside Charles hadn't been extinguished. He blamed Paul Armstrong for Shau Feng's black eye, which had resulted in her being injured. Shau Feng, in her bedroom, couldn't help but hear Sher Sher trying to calm her husband down. He was all for going to Plainfield College to lay Mr. Armstrong out. Charles's voice shook the walls.

"Shau Feng could have been killed in that game!" Shau Feng left the house to run around the grounds with Shau De.

Later, Sher Sher told Shau Feng that the real problem was Charles's seeming dislike for the young man. Laughingly she said, "Your American uncle acts more like a father than a distant relative." Shau Feng had explained to Sher Sher during the flight to Hong Kong about the eye and her pleading with her uncle. Sher Sher sternly stated, "Shau Feng, Charles would never be the same if you had been permanently injured in that game. Did that thought ever enter your mind?" Shau Feng hung her head.

"No, Aunt, I was only thinking about the game."

Sher Sher laughed. "Well, thank God our team won, or Charles would never have forgiven you."

When Diana arrived for the weekend, she brought with her a verbal message from Paul, which she gave to Shau Feng. In the living room, Shau Feng said quietly that she never wanted to see Paul again. Sher Sher suggested that Shau Feng should hear him out.

Diana said, "I think the wisest solution is to hear what he has to say. Paul can't come in person. Your Uncle Charles would harm him. It could result in a lawsuit or worse. What if it got into the papers? After all, it was your wish to keep the black eye a secret."

Shau Feng screamed, "Are you against me?" Diana stood peering straight into Shau Feng's eyes.

"My dearest friend, Paul may be very stupid, but you are just as bad and very pigheaded." Shau Feng stared at Diana, and they both began to laugh.

It required some arm-twisting on Sher Sher's part, but finally Shau Feng agreed to see Paul.

Back in the China house on Monday afternoon, Mrs. Chou told Diana over the intercom that Paul was in the reception room and wanted to see her. He had come to hear the results of his request. Diana agreed to see him and patiently explained to Paul that Shau Feng's uncle harbored some anger toward him, and so the situation would require delicate handling. Diana suggested, "Why don't you send out a representative to Shau Feng to pave the way?" Paul declared that he should go himself, but Diana said, "I told Shau Feng that you aren't the crazy man she believes you are. Will you prove me wrong?" Paul wrestled with his feeling for several moments. Then a look of defeat came to his face. Diana touched his arm with her hand. "Paul, use your natural wisdom. It's the only way."

"All right, I agree."

Paul took Diana by surprise when he consented so fast. She glanced at her wristwatch and said, "Paul, I'm going to call right now and arrange a meeting."

"Thank you, Diana."

Diana smiled at Paul and said, "By the way, would you feel insulted if I invited you to have supper with me tonight at Harry Solomon's Deli, and I paid the check?"

He replied, "It would be an honor to dine with you. I will be inside the China House reception room at 7:00 P.M."

Ever since Jim could remember, his dream had been to be a

lawyer. Besides he was a natural leader. For those reasons, Jim's room was packed with his football teammates. On Monday evening, Diana called Jim to accept the role as second for Paul, to explain Paul's actions to Shau Feng. Jim balked at their proposal. He didn't want to be placed in a position where he could lose two good friends. Diana pooh-poohed his protestation by saying what his teammates had been saying, "All for one."

To Diana, he said he would think about it. To the teammates packed in his room, defensively, Jim argued, "Why pick on a minority to do your dirty work?"

Robin replied, "Paul needs the service of your talented tongue. Diana explained to us that Shau Feng's uncle wouldn't let Paul near his house. Mrs. Lemar said it would be madness for Paul to come at this time. Your wild friend doesn't want to wait for Shau Feng to return to college. Only you can help him."

"Why me?"

Harry said, "Shau Feng will talk to you, but not Paul just yet. Why, Diana and Mrs. Lemar didn't say." Jim knew but kept quiet about it.

"How do I explain to Paul if I fail?"

"Phoenix would never refuse to help a friend or let anyone down. Remember what she said, 'Honor, win or lose, and never be afraid to do the right thing.' There are no free rides worth a damn. Why not use this golden opportunity to find out if you're a talker or a lawyer?"

Jim lifted his proud head to reply, "Bring the devil on. I'll spit in his eye for starters. Let me be, while I start to prepare my case."

Thursday at noon, Jim was scheduled to depart for Middletown, by train. The young man got cold feet while dressing. He often stared daggers at Paul, who was sitting in his only chair.

Jim whinnied, "I got more to lose than you have. Both of you are my good friends." Paul dangled his leg over the arm of the chair.

"Do you think that I want to send somebody to talk for me,

instead of going in person to see Shau Feng? Diana vowed that Shau Feng's uncle wouldn't let me get past the front door. She said in no uncertain words that Mr. Lemar would stop me, and neither of the women in the house could physically stop him. Shau Feng, according to Diana, likes you very much. I don't believe she would harm you—at least, not in front of her aunt and uncle."

Jim glared and replied, "Thanks a lot, you backwoods meatball. I really needed that bit of information now, like you need a hole in your thick skull. Sweet Jehovah, it took me months to grow my nails. Now they will be gone before I arrive at Middletown."

Paul rose, "All for one." It was a good thing Jim's stomach couldn't talk. The damn thing was doing flips. Jim tried to recall his prepared speech. His mind was blank. He couldn't remember what he was going to say. He looked upward. "Why me, oh, Lord?" Pointing to Paul, "this slumgudgeon-eater hit Shau Feng, not me." He proceeded to rub Paul's head vigorously with both hands.

"Hey, what are you doing?"

"I want to rub off some of your mazel on me. You could be thrown off a speeding train from a bridge, land in a river of shit, and still emerge smelling like a rose."

"Jim, where did you learn so many Jewish words?"

A smile came to his lips and spread across his face. "While I was in high school, I worked part time in a kosher delicatessen back home. Old Mrs. Katzman, God bless her soul, only spoke Yiddish and was always wishing me good fortune. I need her help now."

Bobby Gold tapped on the door. "Let's move it, Jim. The train will not wait for you." The African-American checked his appearance in the mirror. He crossed himself before leaving his room. Then he gave Paul the bird as he exited.

Jim casually glanced at the faces of the people seated around him in the first-class compartment of the train. His teammates had collected more than enough money for his traveling expenses.

Diana had instructed Jim, "On Thursday evening, at 5:00 P.M., be on the train station platform. A person will be there to pick you up. The Lemars and Shau Feng are expecting you."

Jim was too nervous to eat. He ordered the waiter in the dining car to bring him coffee. He wished he had some of Diana's composure. In his mind, she was a young woman in complete control of herself. He shook his head, "Boy-shy, my ass." To dispel his growing discomfort, Jim repeated words to himself like a mystical incantation. "Shau Feng is Phoenix.... Phoenix is Shau Feng...." Meanwhile Jim watched the poles go by the window. His mind began wandering. "What is Shau Feng really like?" Jim tried to separate fact from fiction. "Why hadn't Shau Feng kicked Paul's ass after he hit her in the eye, in the locker room? How did Shau Feng create the illusion that clouded our minds? Paul was the only one who saw Shau Feng as a girl. Dad told me there are some people born with ESP. Could Paul be one of those special people?" From a recess inside his mind came a memory full blown. It was something Shau Feng had once said to him as they walked to the football field to practice.

"To snatch the pearl of wisdom from the sleeping dragon's mouth requires much courage and a strong heart. It's not a task to be undertaken by weaklings." The young man said, "Thanks, oh, Lord, I needed that."

The sedan carried Jim through the double gates, which automatically opened at the car's approach. Jim, at the front door, walked the short flight of stone steps and rang the bell. The massive double doors looked freshly painted. A gust of cold air touched the back of his unprotected neck, sending a chill through him. He hoped it wasn't an omen. Jim looked around him and concluded, "The Lemars are very wealthy people." A Chinese woman opened the door. There were still butterflies in his stomach. He said, "Mr. Jim Hawkins to see Miss Shau Feng Chen."

"You are expected, sir." Jim stepped inside the house, and the woman closed the door. "May I have your coat?" He removed it and handed it to the woman. The maid hung his coat in a closet. "Sir, this way, please."

Charles was on his feet as Jim was ushered into the room. The room was a library, lined with books. Jim extended his hand in response to Charles's outstretched hand. It was too late; he hadn't caught Sher Sher's eye in time. She was to his right, vigorously shaking her head. Jim's hand was caught in a viselike grip, being crushed. The pain made him realize Charles Lemar's great strength.

"Good evening, Mr. Hawkin."

"Good evening, Mr. Lemar." Charles released the young man's hand after casting a glance at his wife. Jim tried not to show the man that his hand was almost broken. Diana hadn't exaggerated about what this man could do to Paul. Mrs. Lemar was seated, looking very beautiful in a multicolored dress. Jim said, "Good evening, Mrs. Lemar." Her eyes seemed to say, *I tried to warn you.*

"Good evening, Mr. Hawkin. How was your trip?"

"Fine, thank you." In his mind was *Great, at least she is on my side.* Now he turned to face Shau Feng. Jim saw a younger version of Mrs. Lemar. Shau Feng was dressed in a dark-green suit, a bright-yellow blouse, with lace at the neck, and a three-inch medallion pinned to her jacket. It was a painted Phoenix. Jim gave her his winning smile. He saw the outline of her breast stretching the jacket.

"Shau Feng, you look very beautiful."

"Thank you, Mr. Hawkins. You look very handsome." Jim studied her face for any clues as to what was in her mind. He saw nothing but a smile. Charles indicated where he should sit.

"Mr. Hawkins, would you like a drink?"

"Yes, sir, white wine please." Jim didn't know why he ordered wine; he was a beer drinker. The young man peered at Sher Sher, seeking help. With a nod of her head, she indicated to Jim to start his pitch. In came the maid with his wine, chilled. Jim asked if he could speak to Shau Feng alone.

Shau Feng recrossed her legs, saying, "Anything you wish to say to me can be said in front of my uncle and aunt." His eyes briefly went to Charles, wishing the big man were miles away. Jim fixed his eyes on Shau Feng. He considered the remark Shau Feng had made. *After we mentioned that there were no girls present during the football practice, Shau Feng had quipped that we were blind.* The young lady had completely fooled everyone but Paul. Jim broke off his chain of thought. He was getting himself in a loop. Reaching for the wine glass, he emptied it for Dutch courage.

He rose to his feet. A quick glance towards Shau Feng indicated she wasn't making this easy for him. Her face was now devoid of her usual smile.

"Shau Feng . . . " He paused, finding his voice too high. He brought it down to normal. "I hope you will understand what I'm about to tell you." He could hear himself say inside his head, *Okay, I have her attention. Come on, Phoenix, old buddy. Loosen up and give this horse a break.* He said, "Shau Feng, Paul is in love with you. People in love tend to act a little crazy. This male image you projected tied his emotions in knots, because intuitively he experienced you as a female, but didn't know why. Being clumsy, he badly mishandled the relationship. What really counts is that Paul honestly cares for you. Having conflicting feelings for you drove him wild. Please don't judge him too harshly for his behavior, Shau Feng. Look into your compassionate heart, and remember, he is still your good friend." Jim finished his speech and waited for a reply. Shau Feng's lack of reaction disheartened him. There was a taste of the bitterness of defeat in his mouth, and Jim didn't like it. Angrily he told himself, "Phoenix and Shau Feng are two different people. This was my best shot, and it fell short." Jim had to fight the sudden desire to run away.

Finally Shau Feng said, "Mr. Hawkins, please excuse me for being impolite. I must straighten out something you have just said in my mind, in a language in which I'm comfortable." The young woman faced her aunt and began a dialogue in rapid Chinese. When it was over, Mrs. Lemar invited Jim to have supper with them. Still Shau Feng gave Jim no indication of her thoughts. He peered at his watch and nodded his head. It had occurred to Jim that he hadn't eaten since breakfast.

Charles rose, inquiring if the youth would like to wash before the meal. He mumbled, "Yes, sir."

Jim reentered the room, finding them all on their feet. Shau Feng was talking to her aunt in a low voice. Mr. Lemar appeared like a Titan, towering over the women. Standing side by side, Shau Feng and Mrs. Lemar looked like mother and daughter to Jim. Charles ushered them all into the dining room. This time, the big man's hand was gentle upon Jim's back.

Jim sat next to Sher Sher and across from Shau Feng and Charles. A golden retriever entered the dining room and caught Jim's eye. The big dog sat between Jim and his mistress. He smelled the air and stationed himself facing Jim. Sher Sher rubbed the dog's head. Shau De watched Jim through half-closed eyes. The food platters were placed on the table. To Jim, they looked like pictures. Sher Sher explained to Jim the contents of each dish, and how it was spiced. She pointed out the different sauces, which were used to enhance the food's flavor. To Jim, this Chinese cuisine wasn't like his usual order in a restaurant. During the meal, Charles drew Jim out about his future aspirations. Shau Feng quietly ate her meal, and Jim couldn't make eye contact with her. When tea was served, the young man addressed Shau Feng.

"Miss Shau Feng Chen, do I have something to tell Mr. Armstrong?"

Sitting erect in her chair and looking directly into his eyes, she replied, "Yes, Mr. Jim Hawkins, I will speak to Mr. Armstrong in private, after dinner. I believe I owe him that much." Everyone rose after dessert and retired to the den for after-dinner brandy and coffee.

There was small talk and light banter for a while, until Jim rose. They thanked him for coming. Charles and Sher Sher walked Jim to the door. Shau Feng was at his side. A sharp pain in Jim's ribcage announced that Shau Feng's elbow had struck him. He winced. In a very low voice, Shau Feng said, "Jim, you overgrown dope, you have been hanging around Paul too long. His stupidity has begun to rub off on you. Do you realize that you forgot to offer us your condolences? Why must you eat like a pig? Your body doesn't need that much nourishment. How could you dominate the entire conversation at the table, not allowing others a chance to talk? For the future, you had better brush up on your table manners."

Jim chuckled to himself. *Behind that female paraphernalia, and under that ladylike exterior, lies the real Phoenix. I'll wager if she took a drink of water this minute, it would turn into steam. This young woman is all fire inside. Paul, Shau Feng will burn your ass. Oh, Lord, thank you. There is justice in this world. Friend Paul, you will get a taste of what you have put me through to date for you.*

The trio retired to the den. Shau De raced ahead of Sher Sher into the room. He lay by Sher Sher's favorite chair, sniffing the air. When she came into the room and sat next to Shau Feng, the dog closed both eyes. Charles, standing abruptly, declared, "Ladies, I don't believe I'm needed here. Shau Feng, use your Chen head." Before Jim arrived, Sher Sher had extracted a promise from Charles to keep his thoughts about Paul Armstrong to himself. She didn't want him to pass any remarks about Mr. Armstrong in front of Jim. Shau Feng ran to Charles, throwing her arms around him. He patted her back.

"Uncle, I love you dearly. I'm sorry for all the agony I caused you."

"All is forgiven, Shau Feng." Looking over at his wife, he said, "Love, you look very beautiful tonight."

"Thank you, Dear, I will see you upstairs. I won't be long."

After Charles left, Shau Feng asked, "Auntie, have I unwittingly reopened Uncle's old wound? I wasn't aware of how his old friends had died. All I wanted was to prove that women can play football as equals to men. I had no intention of hurting Uncle Charles."

Sher Sher said, "Your uncle's boyhood friends' death is a painful experience that still bothers him." She bit her lips, rose, and turned her back on Shau Feng. Her head was lowered, and was very quiet. After a few minutes, she started to speak. "Shau Feng, I'm sorry, this entire madness was all my fault. Charles and I never had children, because I was afraid to be like my mother, who died an early death. I know that my spirit would never have allowed me to rest if I left young, motherless children. When Father called about you, I made up a story about Charles wanting only male children. Father misinterpreted what I had said, and he taught you how to act like a boy, to please your American uncle. He was an excellent teacher. After you arrived and I got to know you, I became afraid that I would do or say something to drive you away. Both Charles and I love you very much." Sher Sher covered her face with her hands.

The sound of Shau De's cries made Sher Sher turn around to see what was upsetting the dog. Astonished, she found Shau Feng kowtowing. She said in Chinese, "What are you doing? Get up!" Shau Feng avowed, in Chinese, "I'm an unlucky child, and my parents sent me away. Grandfather should have been enjoying the fruits of his old age. Instead, because of my arrival, he had to look after me. You and Uncle, I owe more than I can ever repay in a lifetime."

Sher Sher lifted the young woman to her feet. She enfolded Shau Feng in her arms. With a finger, she wiped the tears from Shau Feng's eyes.

"Oh, My Dearest One, how mistaken you are! Your parents loved you more than life itself. When they had your horoscope compiled by a monk, they wouldn't let their love for you stand in your way. Your loving parents sent you to your grandfather, who was capable of helping you. Father was well aware of his responsibility when he chose to accept you. As for your uncle, he isn't a weakling, cowed by ghosts. Nobody goes through life untouched by some personal tragedy. This affair with Mr. Armstrong is your own business, and you have to work it out yourself." Sher Sher felt Shau Feng's warm cheek against hers. She took the girl's face between her hands and peered into her eyes. They smiled at each other. Sher Sher tilted her head, saying, "It's a custom among our people to adopt a son or daughter when you are childless. How would you like to be my daughter?"

Shau Feng replied, "Yes, with all my heart, Mother."

Sher Sher was delighted. She kissed the young woman's lips. "It's done, sealed with a kiss of motherly love."

Shau Feng kissed her back. "Until death do us part, Mother."

Her new mother said, "Shau Feng, it's late. Good night, Dear Daughter."

"Good night, Mother." Up sprang Shau De, to follow his mistress.

Lying on the oversized bed in pajamas, Charles watched his wife toss coins into an open dish. She repeated this action several times, and each time she consulted an I Ching book. Charles playfully called out, "Is that Chinese sorcery, or are you casting a magical spell?"

Sher Sher replied, without looking up, "Dear, remember telling me how you use to enjoy eating quarterbacks for breakfast? Well, I believe you could be getting another opportunity." Charles leaped to his feet, roaring, "I won't have it! I'll tear his goddamn head off! Shau Feng is too good for the likes of him. That son-of-a-bitch could have gotten her killed."

Sher Sher retorted, as if speaking to a child, "Charles, you are Shau Feng's American uncle, yet you act more like a father to her. Please refrain from interfering with the young ones. Didn't you promise me to let them settle their differences?" Charles's face didn't change.

Sher Sher asked Charles, "Can't you control your temper, old man? Now promise me again, without crossing your fingers, to let nature take its course."

"Woman of my life," he cried, "Why are you always able to see through me—to the very core of my heart?"

"Maybe it's because I love you so much—and maybe it's because I think you'd make a terrific grandfather for their son."

"Come here, woman of my life, and show me how much you love me. But I still don't like Mr. Armstrong one bit."

In the library, Shau Feng kicked off her shoes and tucked her legs under her, while she sat on the chair. Her thoughts centered on Jim's words. *Paul is in love with you.* Trying to sort out her feelings, she thought, "How can someone be in love with you, when you don't know if you are in love with him? Aren't both people supposed to fall in love with each other at the same time? Anyway, this love business isn't what I had in mind as a relationship between us." A pleasant memory came into her mind. It was the wild run across the campus to Tabard's. "It was fun," she thought, "but can I love a young man who isn't Chinese? Blind man, frog-in-a-well, why can't you leave well enough alone? I thought people in love are supposed to be happy. Why did I feel so miserable seeing Paul with Rita? Diana said that Paul had recently changed—in what way? Paul, this mess is all *your* fault for causing me all these problems."

While Jim was on the train heading for Middletown, Paul was stretched out on his bed, staring at the ceiling. He focused his mind on Shau Feng to soothe the ache in his heart. Paul tried to think of the first time he had known for certain that Phoenix was a female. He came to realize that he had never trusted his intuitive feelings, but clouded his mind by blaming his own inadequacy. He came to understand that he had sensed Phoenix's femaleness all along, but had refused to trust what he sensed. With that veil gone from his mind, all became clear.

"I'm an idiot!" he said to himself. "I'm the blind man that Shau Feng referred to in her allegory. I have always felt that Phoenix was a young woman, but I never trusted my intuition." His hand reached for the jade Buddha on the chain around his neck that Shau Feng had given him as a token of friendship. It pained him to think that if Jim failed, Shau Feng would refuse to speak to him. Her face entered his mind, and Paul said what was in his heart: "Shau Feng, I love you."

Plainfield College organized a committee to plan their National Football Championship celebration. Dr. Oriello's office was packed with representatives from the town, the alumni, the student body, and local and national businessmen. Chet Harris was to be honored as Coach of the Year. He would distribute the National Championship rings to the Lions players.

Mr. Laluma was hired to provide the music for the celebration. The local popular D.J. had a collection of thousands of various tapes to satisfy the taste of just about everyone. The big plus was the man's first-class sound system. He was located in the uppermost tier of seats in the basketball court, adjacent to the TV crew.

A fine powdery snow covered the ground. The brisk wind moved the frozen fluffy snow to pile up against the buildings. The outside temperature dropped to zero. The rear gate to the college was closed. Admission to the college's celebration was by invitation only, because of limited space in the basketball court. Stationed around the front gate to the campus were the state police. The reporters had been chosen by lottery to cover the event.

Every seat inside the basketball court was filled, as was the section for standing room. Mr. Laluma played music while the crowd waited for the ceremony to begin. In the center of the court, on a raised dias, sat the football players, Chet, his wife, and Dr. Oriello. One seat, however, was vacant. Rumors were circulating about whether or not Miss Shau Feng Chen was going to attend.

The television crew was on the topmost tier, near Mr. Laluma. The Division and National Championship banners, separated by an American flag, hung from the ceiling over the television crew. The governor of Ohio was seated among the college's alumni. With a signal from Dr. Oriello, the national anthem was played, and all were on their feet.

Outside the campus a limo entered and drove to the basketball court. Because of a flat tire, the big car was late in arriving. Hurriedly, three people exited the car and walked to the nearest entrance. Once inside, Shau Feng removed her overcoat, remarking that they had come in the wrong door. Sher Sher glanced about, removing her coat. She asked Shau Feng if they should go outside and come in the right door. The girl shook her stubborn head. Sher Sher calculated that there was no way Shau Feng could walk around this dense crowd to her seat. To reach the dais, she would have to walk across the center area of the basketball courts.

Shau Feng wore a bright-red Chinese chi pau dress, which clung to her body. A modest slit at either side showed that she was indeed a young woman. The red high-heeled shoes matched her dress. Long, pale-jade earrings hung from her lobes, and around her neck hung a medallion of a phoenix on a gold chain. Shau Feng's short black hair was very curly. She complained to Sher Sher, who was eyeing the crowd, that her dress was too tight.

"Everything sticks out," she whispered.

Charles, holding the women's coats, nodded his head, thinking, "And all in the right places."

When Chet had finished his speech, Sher Sher caught Charles's eye, indicating for him to plow a path through the crowd to the rope. They followed closely as Charles shouldered people aside. Sher Sher reminded Shau Feng to walk slowly in her dress and high heels, since the floor was highly waxed. Charles kissed his niece on the forehead, raised the rope with his hand, and shoved her out onto the court. Once in the open, Shau Feng had no choice, but to go on.

Mr. Laluma was high on drugs, grooving to the music blaring in his headset. He and the reporter from the TV camera crew were casting cow eyes at each other. The drugs made the man bolder. Leaning forward to blow the young woman a kiss, his elbow activated the speaker switch. Ms. Granger was supervising the TV crew. When she saw Shau Feng walking in the open, she slapped the cameraman on the back and pointed to the young Chinese woman in the red dress.

"That is Shau Feng Chen. Ronny, keep her on camera."

The music blared over the loudspeakers, drowning out the applause. The singer's words bounced around the hall. "I can see you clearly now...." Shau Feng was startled and increased her pace. Being unaccustomed to wearing a tight Chinese dress and walking in high heels, she slipped and went down on the floor.

Paul's eyes were fastened on Shau Feng. The moment she emerged from the crowd, his heart began to pound and his pulse to throb. When Shau Feng sank to the floor, Paul sprung out of his chair, leaping off the dais to run at breakneck speed across the waxed floor toward Shau Feng.

Diana saw Shau Feng fall and shouted, in Chinese, "Shau Feng, I'm coming to help you!" The students around Diana recognized the Chinese words meaning "Little Phoenix." They immediately came to their feet, roaring her name, and moved into the aisles. Instinctively the entire football team left the dais, running behind Paul. Diana was unable to force her way past the impenetrable bodies clogging the aisles. The crowd was chanting, "Shau Feng, Shau Feng, Shau Feng...." It drowned out the loudspeakers.

Paul assisted Shau Feng to her feet, his hand brushing her skin, which felt cool to his touch. Shau Feng raised her eyes to look at the person who was helping her. She whispered, "I'm all right.

Take your hands off me." To her surprise, Paul did not react to her request. He continued to hold her. "Paul, you damn fool, the audience and public are watching us." Still no response from Paul. The young woman muttered to herself, "I can't knee this American ape in front of everyone." Aloud she called to him, "Oh, Paul, are you there? I'm not hurt. It's these damned high heels. Dummy, let me go this instant!" Shau Feng's words fell upon deaf ears. The Lions players surrounded the couple, separating them from the oncoming crowd. The young men grinned at each other while they listened to Shau Feng scold Paul. Her Chinese name was being echoed throughout the courts. Shau Feng decided to alter her approach, using one that Sher Sher had employed on Charles. A big smile came to her face, and her eyes sparkled. Gently her hands rubbed Paul's arms as she said, "Paul dearest, when are you going to release me?"

The overall effect of her sweet voice and smile devastated Paul. He drew her closer, replying, "Never." Their teammates looked at them with mischief written all over their faces. Paul kissed Shau Feng. She screamed inside her head. Her whole being seemed suddenly on fire.

"Aiya! I will bang his empty head against a tree when I get him alone! In public, before a television audience of millions! I'll punch out his lights, the retard!" Shau Feng felt for the nerve center in Paul's arm and pinched it. At last she was free as Paul's arms dropped to his side. Before she could retaliate, Paul said, "Shau Feng, I truly love you." Suddenly, her repressed feelings of love surfaced. The effect calmed yet excited her. An inner voice was speaking to her, saying, "You are truly a woman now." Warm, tender feelings surged through her, and she took Paul's face in both hands and kissed him.

Watching Paul and Shau Feng kissing, Robin elbowed Stu. "How do you like Paul's grandstand play?"

"It was a dud. Shau Feng stonewalled him on contact."

Charles and Sher Sher witnessed Paul's kissing Shau Feng in

the center of the court. He began to move forward, growling, "I'll hospitalize that guy." Sher Sher, in desperation, grabbed her husband's arm, trying to hold him back. He dragged her effortlessly along with each stride. Sher Sher tried to stop Charles by pinching his arm numerous times as hard as she could. Finally he stopped and looked at her. "Hey, what is that for, girl?"

Sher Sher looked into her husband's eyes. "Dutch, don't you remember what it was like to be in love?" It had been years since she had called him Dutch. He encircled her waist with his arm, pulling her to him. Sher Sher said in an authoritative voice, "Behave yourself, Charles. We are in public." Her eyes widened as his face came closer and closer to her. "Dutch, not here, you great big American Neanderthal." He kissed her lips.

Harry signaled his teammates to separate Shau Feng from Paul. The oncoming mob was almost on top of them, enthusiastically chanting, "Shau Feng . . . Shau Feng . . . " The echo reverberated around the building. From behind their backs, the Plainfield students produced a bouquet of six yellow roses. A student leader had found out from Diana that Shau Feng's grandfather used to say that all Chen women were known as six yellow roses. After many tellings, it came out that Shau Feng's nickname was "Six Yellow Roses." The young people waved the roses like banners to honor their heroine. The Lions team formed a double protective ring around Shau Feng. They had never seen Phoenix dressed as a girl. They wondered, Was this really Phoenix, who had fought with them side by side to win the championship?

Shau Feng smiled warmly at them. She said, "Gentlemen, I saw the rerun of the National Championship game. You were all outstanding. I was of little help."

Harry interrupted her to reply, "Shau Feng, that is incorrect. It was you who were magnificent, like the Statue of Liberty, it was your courage that illuminated the way in our darkest moment." What she had said reassured them that this was indeed their Phoenix. Boyish or ladylike, she was one of them. Some politely asked if she was okay; others shook her hand. Shau Feng, not knowing what else to say, went and hugged them.

Paul, now aware that he was out of the protective circle surrounding Shau Feng, stood facing Jack, a guard who began to tease Paul. "Paul, you blond god, *love* the shade of your lipstick." Joe, standing beside Jack and facing Paul, said, "Doesn't he resemble a lovesick rhinoceros we saw on TV the other day?" Joe replied, "No, Paul looks stupider than that dumb animal. What other exciting feat will you perform today? Will you moon the TV camera?" Art, standing behind Joe and Jack, imitating Paul's voice, said, "Phoenix, I love you." But no amount of harassment from his teammates could dampen Paul's spirit now. Shau Feng's uncle could kill him now, and he would die content.

The football players restrained the eager crowd from getting to Shau Feng. They wanted to touch Shau Feng, hold her hand, and receive a smile from her. A young man, frustrated that he couldn't get near Shau Feng, threw the flowers over the heads of the double ring of football players. They fell at Shau Feng's feet. Others followed his example, throwing the roses and chanting her name. The pile of yellow roses built up. Bronco picked up a handful of flowers and gave them to Shau Feng. Robin told Phoenix, that they were going to lift her up on their shoulders to show her to the audience.

Dr. Oriello and Chet were applauding Shau Feng. Ms. Granger, looking down from her position in the court, wiped a tear from her eye. Paul, concentrating solely on Shau Feng's face, recalled his dream in which he had come to Shau Feng's aid. The dream's meaning suddenly became clear in his mind. It wasn't about Shau Feng's problem but his. The China House symbolized the final hurdle he had to overcome to reach Shau Feng.

"Is Paul the one I saw in my dream, the one who held me in his arms as we danced?" She thought, as she glanced over at Paul. For the first time in his life, Paul was at peace with himself. He had freed himself of the fears that had been haunting him. Shau Feng's kiss had reassured him that they could be more than friends.

Diana was crying from happiness. Bruce handed her his handkerchief. The Chinese students waved banners bearing Shau Feng's name written in Chinese. Charles, holding his wife in his arms thought, "My father-in-law really liked me after all. He sent both his precious possessions to me. I wish we could have had understood each other better."

Bathing in the glory and praise, Shau Feng remembered the one person who had made this all possible. It was too late for her to share the honor with him. The old master was dead and buried. Nevermore would she see his kind face or hear his gentle voice. The loss overwhelmed her as tears streamed down her cheeks. She lowered her head and buried her face in the yellow roses. The sounds of her sobbing, which were low, increased in volume. Everyone was stunned into silence. All that was heard in that quiet basketball court was the music and the singer singing, "I can see you clearly now. . . . " Her teammates lowered the young woman to her feet.

Frantically Paul tried to get to her, but the guys held him back. He was struggling with Jim. "Paul, Shau Feng may be yours forever and ever, but, for today, Phoenix belongs to us all."

Paul cried out in anguish, "Jim, is she all right?"

Jim turned to look at Shau Feng, then looked back to Paul. He playfully slapped Paul's face. "You bet. . . . She is a true champion."

The dance floor was crowded with the young people, the guests, the parents, the faculty, and the visitors. Paul took Shau Feng away from his teammates, who had dominated her company all evening. She excused herself and went with him.

"Shau Feng," he said, "I must know truly how you feel about me. Since that last game, I have been through a lot of changes. I have learned to trust my real feelings. You know that I love you, and I want to be a part of your life. We have cultural differences—but I love you enough to work everything out."

She reached over to take his hand and replied, "I was

engrossed in acting out a male role without giving any thought to love. I think I've always been attracted to you since that evening at the cafeteria. We have a long time ahead of us to get to know each other." They both fell silent. Paul opened his arms, and she came willingly to him. Their bodies touched. They sensed each other's warmth. They looked into each other's eyes and were content. They kissed, and their kiss was more eloquent than any words; it held a promise of the future. He whispered in her ear, "Shau Feng, I adore you." That sound made her heart beat faster, and she touched his face.

"Paul, we are young. I want time for us to get to know each other better. I have my own faults: I'm a hot tempered female—sharp-tongued, stubborn, and strong-willed—but I'm not beyond reason."

"Shau Feng," said Paul, "you overlooked something important. You're very kindhearted and a compassionate human being. I want to apologize for hitting you in the eye. I've read that love reveals itself in many forms, some of which we don't understand." He held her at arms' length, studying her face. "Shau Feng, I don't want our daughter to follow in your footsteps. I want her to be a quarterback—like her father."